TOCABAGA 8

THE INVISIBLES

THOMAS H. WARD

TOCABAGA 8:

THE INVISIBLES

by

THOMAS H. WARD

ISBN-13: 978-0692337936

ISBN-10: 0692337938

Transcendent Publishing
www.transcendentpublishing.com

PREFACE

What does the future hold for America? Read "The Tocabaga Chronicles" to find out what could happen to our wonderful country. Find out how to protect your loved ones and survive the chaos after the apocalypse. We're at war every day fighting evil.

Law and order only exists at the end of a gun. It takes tough hard men and women working as a team to stay safe and free. Friends and family need to stick together to fend off the daily threats of death. You need to be smart, compassionate, and ruthless with those who would do you harm. You need guns, guns, and more guns with a ton of ammunition or you will not survive for very long. Good luck in the future.

China now holds 46 percent of all U.S. debt.

It is the largest holder of all U.S. debt. If the United States cannot repay the debt in an international currency or gold then China could demand payment in tangible property, such as real estate.

If you check history, many lands were sold or given as payment of debt. The United States took over Texas, California, Arizona, and New Mexico after the Mexican-American War as payment. We purchased Alaska from Russia. The U.S. purchased land from France in a deal called the Louisiana Purchase. Spain ceded Florida to the United States in 1821.

The current President put into effect Executive Order 13603 which declared that all property belongs to the Federal Government: your house, money, guns, and even your kids. They can tell you where to live and where to work. If you don't think this can happen, then Google U.S. internment camps.

In 1942 President Roosevelt issued Executive Order 9066 which put over 120,000 Japanese-Americans in camps taking away their freedom and Constitutional rights. This is a fact that many Americans don't know about. German-Americans were also put into camps. The Presidential Order was given because these Americans were deemed a threat by the government. The President has a lot of power and can become a dictator if inclined to do so.

The Military is split over whether to follow the President's orders which violate the U.S. Constitution or to support the people. The regular Army is standing down but the Special Forces, which includes the Army Rangers, Delta Force, Airborne troops, Navy Seals, and other special operations have taken the side of the people and the Constitution. It's a civil war over the rights of the people versus the government.

I am the oldest of three brothers. We grew up fighting bullies and gang members in a tough neighborhood in south Chicago. My Dad, one of the most honest men I have known, always stressed, tell the truth, and help each other. Never, ever be a bully, never steal, and try to protect those who cannot protect themselves. I have always stood up for the people who could not defend themselves. I hate liars and bullies.

Standing 6 feet tall at 180 pounds, I am in great shape for my age and my body is honed by years of physical training. I keep in shape by lifting weights almost every day and running three miles four times a week. I shave my head two times a week as it is cooler in the hot south and wear a ball hat to keep the sun off my head. There's a two inch scar on my forehead from a knife fight years ago.

I spent four years in the Army as a Military

Policeman, and became an expert in the use of handguns, rifles, shotguns, and hand-to-hand combat. My legs have skin grafts from burns received from an explosion when working for the DOD (Department of Defense). I always carry my Glock 17 and Black Bear Cold Steel fighting knife.

I love our country, freedom, my family, and friends. If anyone messes with my family, or my friends, justice will be swift and painful. I have no use for anyone who breaks the law, cheats, or steals. For the most part I follow the Ten Commandments, but also believe in The Code of Hammurabi which is an eye for an eye. I fight to keep our Bill of Rights under the United States Constitution.

I am Director of Security for Tocabaga Island. I live here along with 610 other Patriots. We're fighting to keep our freedom, our homes, and our families safe from the evil forces gone wild. Tocabaga is a sanctuary or safe haven. If you believe in the Constitution, the Bill of Rights, and are of good moral character you are welcome here.

We are waiting for you to contact us by email to find out where Tocabaga is located. Sending us an email is your first step to Freedom. There is an email address at the end of these chronicles. Tocabaga is a real location. I will reply.

My name is, Jack Gunn, and these are my chronicles.

SUMMARY of JULY 9th

and 10th, 2025

Colonel Park, the Chinese commie who befriended me, had disappeared from Fort Desoto sometime during the night. It appeared, by the tracks left in the sand, that he was not alone. He had left the island using a small boat with two other men. I had just put my trust in Park, who was really a Korean by birth, and made him my blood brother. This is an honor I don't bestow on just anyone.

I hate to say it but Tom could be right and Park is still a commie working for the Red Chinese to take over Tocabaga. The Amazon Warriors, along with me, and five of my men, were guarding Fort Desoto beach against a possible invasion by the Reds. We didn't see any signs of that during the day.

It was sometime after midnight when we came under fire from an unknown origin. We made a rapid withdrawal because we were out gunned. Rounds from a rapid-fire 37 mm cannon rained down on us. We knew someone was shooting at us, but we had no idea who or where they were. I suspected it was a Red Chinese gunboat.

JULY 10, 2025 CONTINUED,

SOMETIME AFTER MIDNIGHT

We were on the main road, out of cannon range, driving toward Tocabaga when my radio crackled, "Jack, come in this is Colonel Park." Jim Bo suddenly stopped the truck and we looked at each other in disbelief.

Park radioed, "Jack, you're being invaded. Get off the beach now. Meet me at the campground and I'll fill you in on the details."

The island that Fort Desoto is located on used to have a campground. In the good old days, when things were normal, people would camp for the weekend. It was a beautiful clean campground surrounded by water. Those were the days when you had time to relax. We played baseball and fished for fun. There is no more baseball. We fish to keep from going hungry. There is no more fun.

Jim Bo asked, "What do you wanna do?"

Tommy said, "It's a trap, don't trust him."

"We have no choice. Head to the campground," I ordered. "Tommy, you man the fifty just in case."

I clicked the radio. "Park, we're on the way."

We had no sooner started to move and … KABOOM … a big explosion rocked the Hummer shaking us up. I banged my head on the side of the truck. Lucky for us the old Hummer was still running. Jim Bo floored it to get us out of the line of fire.

Dazed, with blood running down my face, I yelled, "What the hell was that?"

"I think it was an RPG," Tommy replied. "You got a nasty cut on your head."

As we sped away another RPG round whizzed by us and exploded after hitting a tree.

"That was close. Who the hell is shooting at us?" I asked. As we pulled away I could hear bullets pinging off our Hummer.

"I don't know. I can't see anyone," Tommy

shouted, over the sound of the projectiles bouncing off the bullet proof metal.

Our truck was getting hammered by automatic fire, but we couldn't see anyone shooting at us. We sped away to the campground about a mile down the road.

We cautiously pulled up to the old small office and stopped. I took out my bandanna and wiped the blood off my face. Tommy tied it around my head to stop the bleeding.

I dismounted and looked around for Colonel Park, but he wasn't there. I called out, "Park, where are you?" I opened the rotted wooden door to the old one room office and peeked inside.

"There's no one here!"

Tommy, sitting in the machine gun turret, yelled, "See, I told you, it's a trap!" I heard him rack the big 50 caliber machine gun.

I thought, oh no, more FUBAR!

I yelled, "Park, where are you?" There was no reply.

I clicked the radio, "Park, come in."

"Jack, stop yelling. I'm over here."

I spun around but didn't see Park anywhere. "Park, stop playing hide and seek. Where the hell are you?"

"Tell your men to hold their fire and we'll come out," He said.

I yelled, "Hold your fire. Park is coming out."

I was standing right next to the office, near some bushes, when I heard Park say, "I'm right here." I was looking in the direction of his voice when Park's head appeared out of nowhere. It just popped up out of thin air about 20 feet away. The rest of his body was basically invisible.

I looked at him and said, "Holy shit, Batman."

Tommy swung the big fifty around, aiming it at Park, and said. "It's a stealth suit. I used one during the war."

Park walked up to me with another man who also had on an invisible suit with just his head showing. Park said, "Jack, meet Lieutenant Lee. Lee, this is Jack Gunn."

He gave me a slight bow showing respect. "It's my pleasure to meet you, Mr. Gunn."

I returned the bow. "Lieutenant Lee, nice to meet you."

Peering into Park's eyes I said, "You got a lot of explaining to do. What happen to you and where'd you get these invisible clothes?"

"It's a long story Jack. We killed two commies and took their suits. There's also a stealth gunboat in the channel."

"That's what was shooting at us. I knew there was a boat out there. Where are the rest of your men?"

"They're all dead. The commies killed them when they found out General Chen was dead. They blamed us for that. I'll fill you in on the details later. We don't have time to discuss it right now.

"Jack, you have to trust me. You need to set up a defensive line because they're coming."

"Who's coming? Somebody was shooting at us on the way over here. Who are these guys?" I asked.

"They're a stealth Chinese Special Forces platoon, called the 'Invisibles'. These guys are badass and are considered the best of the best."

Tommy and I studied the suits close up. You could see the outline of the suits from fifteen feet away. Touching the fabric it felt like glass or plastic and had a very rough surface.

Tommy commented, "These are almost the same as the one I wore. The commies probably copied them. They're uncomfortable and hot as hell."

I nodded at Tommy. "I remember the first invisible suits were used in Afghanistan in 2013. The original idea came from an old movie called 'The Predator'. How do these things work?"

Tom replied, "I'm not an Engineer, so I don't know exactly. They're made using nanotechnology. I think they're some kind of nano-glass. Each piece is like a nano-picture tube which shows the background all around you. It's interlaced with carbon nano-tubes which act as the transmitter or nano-camera. You become totally invisible 360 degrees around the suit. The most important part is the mini-computer that operates the thing. I was told each one costs around 10 million bucks to make."

I walked around the suit looking at it and asked, "What powers it?"

"Tiny atomic batteries," Park said.

"What happens if they get wet?"

"Rain affects the suit and makes it unstable. It could flicker on and off."

I asked, "Park, what should we do?"

"I suggest you pull back to the bridge with your men and dig in on this side. Lee and I will get behind them. Then we'll pick them off one by one."

Tommy commented, "We'll make some ad

hoc ghillie suits. The camouflage will make it difficult to spot us."

I asked, "Can these invisibles see each other?"

Park answered, "Yes and no. They keep in contact by radio with position finders that are like a GPS. It's built into the helmet."

I said, "So they know where each man is at all times."

"Yes, unless the GPS is turned off."

"Here's a stupid question. How can we see these guys before they see us?"

Park gave me a weird smile. "We'll be your eyes. I'll radio you their position."

Tommy spoke up. "There's two other methods to detect them. One is using radar and the other is laser beams. Since they're solid objects the radar will detect them. A red laser beam will bounce off the nano glass and reflect a red glow. The problem is they're only good for a couple of hundred yards."

Tommy pointed his M4 laser at Park's suit and it glowed a faint, but much larger than normal red dot. It wasn't very bright, but you could see it in the dark.

Park commented, "I never knew that. You

learn something new every day."

I said, "All our M4s have lasers, so that solves the problem. However, if they see our lasers they can get a fix on our location. It'll be a question of who shoots first."

Tommy said, "Not necessarily. Mike and I could snipe them from the trees so they might not spot us. We'll scan the area with the lasers and when we spot the reflection we'll shoot the bastards."

"Yeah, that sounds reasonable."

Tommy advised, "Here's what I suggest. We position ourselves just after the intersection, where the road splits off to the old boat ramps. Mike will be on one side of the street in a tree and I'll be on the other. The four of you spread out; two on each side of the street. Stick some twigs and grass in your clothes to create some camouflage. Then find a spot with good protection."

I added, "Jim Bo and I will take the westside of the road. Tony, Rick, you take the east."

We all agreed on the plan. As we mounted up I said, "Park, be careful out there. I don't want to shoot you by mistake."

Park said, "Don't worry. We'll be careful." Park and Lee disappeared after putting on their invisible cloth covered helmets. I noticed that I could see their rifles, which were not invisible. I made a mental note of that.

On the way to the south side of Shark Channel Bridge I radioed Amy that we were approaching and filled her in on the details about the invisibles soldiers. I advised her to use lasers to detect them.

The Amazons would stay on the north side of the bridge using cars for a road block. This road block would be the last line of defense. If these soldiers made it past us they would never make it past the 20 Amazons. There is only one way to get past the Amazons and that's to swim across Shark Channel or take a boat. A boat is an easy target for my shooters.

Tommy commented, "I still don't trust Park."

"I agree," Jim Bo said. "I could tell that Lee didn't like us just by looking at his face. It showed a lot of hatred."

I replied, "We'll find out pretty soon if they can be trusted."

Reaching our sniper location we quickly dismounted. I turned to Jim Bo. "Back the Hummer into the jungle next to that old sign and cover it up with leaves. Stay in the gun turret so you'll have a better view."

Mike and Tommy scampered up tall trees on each side of the street. Tony and Rick went to the east side and hid behind some mangrove bushes at the edge of the water. We were all in position.

I trotted back down the road about 100 feet and stopped. Using my naked eyes I searched for each one of my hidden men. I figured if I could see them then the enemy could see them. They were well hidden so I was satisfied and returned to my position.

I hunkered down under the sign which used to say 'Boat Ramps'. It was supported by two, five-foot-tall concrete pillars. Jim Bo, sitting in the gun turret, was about 15 feet away.

I got on the radio. "Park, we're all in position. What's your status and where's the enemy? Over."

"They're slowly coming towards you. I guess they're about 500 meters away from you. Out."

I looked at my watch it was just past 4 am when I heard four shots. My radio came on. "Jack, we just killed two. Park, out."

I was really hoping that Park and Lee would terminate at least half of the Invisibles before they reached our location. I heard five shots and then automatic gunfire from an AK47.

My radio hissed. "We got two more. Over."

"Park, what was the automatic fire about?"

"Oh, that was Lee. He got carried away. They just turned off their GPS locators. We have to sit tight for a while. Over and out."

It was spooky sitting there in the moon-light waiting for invisible soldiers to attack us. I could see Tommy and Mike's lasers scanning the area. We were all on edge waiting for the red glow to appear.

My trigger finger was twitching. It wanted to shoot someone. I started talking to my finger. "Settle down boy, settle down." I took my hand off the grip and made a fist several times. I was tense and needed to let off some steam.

Muttering to myself I said, "Come on, you commie bastards."

I whispered to Jim Bo, "Don't shoot that fifty unless I tell you where to shoot at. Those rounds can go a mile and I don't wanna shoot Park by mistake."

"Ok Boss, whatever you say, but I'm using the M4 anyway. I couldn't hit shit with that machine gun."

"Good idea. Let me know if you see anything." Since Jim Bo was sitting in the gun turret he would most likely see a red glow before I would.

I looked at the eastern sky and could tell the sun would be up soon. The moon was almost gone. Peering out into the darkness I could see our lasers flashing on the edge of the jungle. Then I heard Jim fire a shot. The sudden bang from a few feet away made me jump.

I said, "Damn Jim, warn me when you gonna shoot."

"Sorry, but I saw two red spots. I think I hit one of them but the other disappeared."

"Where?"

"They were on the edge of the jungle, right near the road going to the boat ramp. They're gone now."

I pointed my laser at the area, about 200 feet away, and didn't see a damn thing. "Keep scanning that area," I advised.

The big problem, when scanning the area, everything showed a red dot. If the beam hit a tree, leaf, or anything the red dot was there. The only difference was the dot on the invisible suit was bigger, and not so well defined or bright. Maybe Jim didn't see anything but a tree or animal.

I hadn't heard a peep out of Park for about an hour so I keyed my radio. "Park, what's going on?" There was no reply.

Mike came on the radio. "Hey guys, I spotted something over here. I think three invisibles are 200 feet in front of me."

I cocked my head out from behind the concrete pillar and could see three faint red spots. Tony came over the radio. "We got them painted. Fire!" A wall of gunfire hit the red dots and they fell to the ground. Not one of them fired a round at us.

Then it occurred to me that the two jerks Jim saw might be headed to the boat ramp. That would enable them to get behind us or make it to the bridge. I decided to leave my sniper position and check if Jim really saw anything.

I got on the radio, "Everyone, listen up. I'm heading to the boat ramps. Jim saw two men moving in that direction. So don't shoot me by mistake."

Jim said, "I'll come along and cover your back."

"Ok." I keyed my radio, "Jim Bo is with me. Tommy, you need to watch our section."

Tommy answered, "Affirmative. Be careful

it's a jungle out there." We laughed because that's an expression I always use.

We followed the edge of the woods to the road. Jim took one side of the street and I took the other. The trees were towering high on each side of the road blocking any moon-light.

Jim commented, "Man, it's dark here. What's the plan?"

"You just keep checking behind us for anyone. If these guys are here they could ambush us. The plan is simple … we terminate them."

After progressing about 500 feet along the road I raised my hand signaling Jim to stop. I waved him over to me and whispered, "I don't see anything. Let's just stay here a minute and listen."

We both dropped to one knee and didn't move a muscle. Our ears were straining to hear the slightest noise. I was squinting trying to see if anything, a bush or tree, was moving. Peering into the dark shadowy jungle your eyes play tricks on you. You imagine that you saw something when you didn't.

My sixth sense told me they were close. Then I heard it and so did Jim Bo. It was the soft snap of a twig. It was just one snap, but I knew it was them. Most animals living in this jungle aren't big enough to snap twigs on the ground. Jim Bo and

I both instantly looked in the direction of the noise.

Jim said, "Did you hear that?"

I whispered very softly, "Don't move. Stay down."

I flipped off my safety and aimed my M4 in that direction while looking through my FLIR scope. I squeezed the laser button and started to paint the area.

Nothing was there, but I heard the bushes move and more twigs snapping and it was getting closer to us. The undergrowth was very thick. It was so thick that a man could be walking or crawling through it undetected. I saw the tops of the 4 foot tall ferns start to sway. It was coming directly towards us and it was coming fast.

Jim Bo and I both pointed our guns at the movement. Suddenly a huge blur burst out of the dense bushes attacking Jim. It knocked him to the ground while making growling like sounds.

I pumped ten rounds into the belly of the monster. The huge creature turned and ran towards me like a charging bull. I shot it five times in the head as it lunged at me. The creature skidded to a stop on its belly, dead at my feet.

The damn thing scared the shit out of me. My hands were shaking as I looked at the giant wild boar. It had to be 300 pounds and 3 feet high.

"It got me good … in the leg," Jim said, while holding his leg, in obvious pain.

I bent down to look at the wound in Jim's calf muscle. The boar's long tusks had sliced it wide open. He had a five inch cut that was bleeding severely. Jim needed immediate medical attention. I took his belt and tied it just above the knee to help stop the bleeding.

I asked, "Can you walk?"

"I think so." I grabbed his arm and helped him stand up. I slung both weapons as he put his arm around my shoulder. We slowly started to hobble back to our defensive line.

After a few steps, I said, "This isn't gonna work." I got on the radio. "Tommy, Jim got attacked by a wild boar. Get the Humvee and pick him up."

"Ok, be right there." We sat down in the road while I kept watch for any other surprises. I was worried that the Invisibles may have heard the shots.

Tommy pulled up and dismounted. While observing the pig, he asked, "That's what the gunfire was all about?"

"Yeah, we killed a pig."

"What happened?"

I told him, "That damn thing charged out of the jungle and managed to slice Jim and almost got me." I walked over to the giant ugly thing and gave it a good kick. "That's biggest piggy I ever saw."

Wild hogs are disgusting looking animals that have long hair growing on their bodies. They are strong and the males have big sharp tusks. They eat anything, including people. No one knows how they got here, but these opportunistic omnivores wreak havoc on the land and agriculture. They live all over Florida.

We loaded Jim into the front seat. I told Tom. "Take him to Amy. She'll know what to do."

Amy is Jim's wife, Commander of the Amazon Warriors, and she's a trauma nurse. Jim Bo will be in good hands. Looking at Jim I could tell he was going into shock.

Jim Bo is my nick name for Jim. He's a great guy who married my only daughter. He has a good heart and is loyal to the core. I love him like my own son. He keeps his word and is fully trustworthy. I know he would give his life to protect his family and that of Tocabaga.

Jim has black hair and blue eyes. He stands 6'2" and comes in around 185 pounds of solid muscle. He works out and runs with me all the time. He's an expert in the use of weapons from years of training with the Gunn family.

"Are you coming?" Tom asked.

"No, I'm staying here. I wanna find the two guys Jim saw," I replied.

"Are you sure?"

"Yeah, I'll be fine. Get going."

"Ok, but don't take any chances. Radio me if you need help."

I stood there watching Tommy drive off leaving me on the dark lonely road. Soon they were out of sight. A shiver ran down my spine knowing I was alone.

I crept forward walking on the edge of the road near the jungle. It was a slow process because I had to keep using my laser to scan the area. I'd move 20 feet then get down on one knee and shoot the laser beam around. I had to keep checking behind me in case an Invisible was lurking.

I reached the overgrown grass covered parking lot, which is the end of the road. Dropping to one knee I took a drink of water before proceeding. The damn mosquitoes were eating me up. I hate that buzzing sound when they fly around your head.

Gazing around the parking lot it looked all clear, but the grass was so high it was hard to tell. My plan was to move along the edge of the woods to Shark Channel Bridge. If the Chinese were here they would be doing the same thing. This would allow them to move behind our lines and attack us from the rear. From here it was probably about half a mile to the bridge.

I sat there still gazing and listening. Shortly the sun would break the horizon. I wondered if we could see the Invisibles in the day light. The laser beams wouldn't be as effective. I thought how in the hell will we be able to spot them in the bright sun light? I had to move out. I checked my M4, putting in a new magazine, and racked in a fresh round.

As I proceeded the bushes move, about 100 feet away, directly in my path. Hogs are usually in groups so there could be more of them around here. I aimed my laser in that direction, but only saw trees and bushes.

Then a warning went off in my head. My adrenalin started to pump. My hands started to shake a little as I came closer and closer to the location where the bushes moved. I thought, calm down, it's probably nothing.

Ten feet away I stopped and stared at the area. I admit the darkness, combined with the thought of Invisibles, was really getting to me. I froze in my steps thinking I heard a noise.

Aiming the laser directly in front of me, I squeezed the on button located on the hand guard. Nothing happened so I squeezed harder. There wasn't any beam.

I whispered, "Shit." Taking off my Nomex gloves, I unslung my M4. Reaching into my tiny vest pocket, I felt around for a battery. Pulling it out I knelt down to remove the laser and quickly change the battery.

I thought I heard a noise to my right. As I pivoted to look … WHACK! The lights went out for a second as I tumbled backwards dropping my rifle. Somehow I managed to stand up to see who hit me in the face.

I didn't see anything, but a blur, and then … WHACK! Another strong blow hit me in the chest knocking the wind out of me. I was lucky I had on my BPV (bullet proof vest) underneath my tactical vest otherwise the blow could have broken some ribs.

WHACK … another blow to my face knocked me on my back to the ground. My nose started to bleed profusely. I saw a blur again and felt a sharp kick to my head. I guessed there would be another, so I reached out and grabbed the foot I could barely see.

I twisted the foot, with both hands, as hard as I could. He fell next to me. I could feel the sharp jagged glass texture of the invisible suit. Being this close I could make out the suit. I grabbed him and pulled myself on top, while holding him down with all my strength and weight, as he flailed away at my face.

I mounted him for a classic ground and pound move. I got in two good punches to his body, but his helmet deflected my punch to his face. He swung his right leg up, hooking me around the neck, and flipped me backwards.

Sitting on my butt, I drew my Glock and pointed it … BAM … BAM. The semi-invisible man plunged on top of me.

Pushing the Invisible off, I quickly removed his helmet revealing his head. He coughed and whispered, "You got me, blood brother."

"Park, what the hell are you doing? It's me, Jack!"

"I knew it was you. I was going to … kill you." He let out a little laugh. Blood sprayed out of his mouth indicating a round had hit his lungs.

"Why kill me? Doesn't friendship mean anything to you?" I asked.

"I'm a Communist … first and foremost." Park hesitated and said, "We're sworn enemies."

"Then why did you kill General Chen?"

"To make you trust me. Besides, I hated that … fat ass." Park coughed up more blood.

"Why did you show us the stealth suits and advise us what to do?"

"It was all a trap … to lure you in."

I commented, "So the Invisibles are really your men."

"I'm the … Commander," Park said, while coughing up dark red ooze.

He continued to speak, but I could hardly hear him so I leaned in closer. "Thanks, for an honorable death. Watch out … for … Lee." He let out one last breath and that was it for my traitor blood brother. I pushed his eyes shut with my index finger.

I felt sad, not for myself, but for him. He couldn't change his thinking. He couldn't accept freedom. He couldn't accept a true friend. That's what communism does to you.

I wondered why Park didn't shoot me.

Maybe he wanted to prove he could beat me in hand-to-hand combat since he never graduated from Mr. Yoon's fighting school. I'll never know now. I quickly glanced around looking for Lee.

It occurred to me that I could use Park's stealth suit to hunt down Lee and the other Invisibles. I had to be careful however, because my own men could shoot me.

I dragged Park's body to Shark Channel; wrestled off his suit and put it on. The stealth suit was flexible like a spandex material. The inside was smooth and it fit me with no problem.

As I placed the cloth covered helmet over my head tiny LED lights appeared on heads up display. The helmet had a built in camera. There was Chinese writing, which I didn't understand. Tommy was right the suit was heavy and hot as hell. I was being smothered and couldn't breathe.

It was too restricting and my claustrophobia was kicking in. I ripped off the helmet. Looking down at Park I rolled his body into the dark water. I stood there for a minute, and watched it float away while wiping the blood from my nose. It didn't take long for shark fins to appear.

Park could have easily killed me. I'll never know why he didn't, but maybe, just maybe, he did like his blood brother. Maybe my friendship did rub off on him.

Killing my so-called blood brother brought back memories from a long time ago. I was just 16 years old and had many blood brothers because we were all part of the same gang. Our gang was nicknamed 'The Good Guys' by the local neighborhood people because we stole from the bad guys and gave back what they had taken. We helped the needy and poor old people. It sounds stupid, but that's what we did.

We didn't permit pushers or drug dealers in our territory. None of us took drugs except some smoked a little pot or drank a beer every now and then. We were tough guys who protected our neighborhood from the evil-doers. Anyone who came to our neighborhood, to cause problems, do shake downs for protection money, or sell hard core drugs to kids, got a lesson from us. We called ourselves the Dirty Dozen, named after a movie, because there were 12 of us. The cops were our friends. They never bothered us much because we kept the neighborhood safe and crime free.

If a kid or neighbor told us that there was a pusher selling drugs we would all confront him. We'd take his drugs and throw them down the street sewer. We'd take his money and beat the shit out of him. One of our favorite methods to deal with them was to break their knee caps with a ball-peen hammer. That was very painful and it would put them out of action for months.

The Mob didn't mind what we did either because a few of them lived around our hood and didn't want their kids or family to be victims of the dirtbags. So we pretty much had a green light to do whatever was needed to make our hood safe. All the other local criminal gangs didn't dare infringe into our space.

Members in our gang had known each other since grade school. We were real blood brothers. It was a closed society since we didn't permit new members. One of my best friends was Mickey. I saved Mickey's ass many times over the years, as he did mine.

I stopped at the local deli for a sandwich after school one day. Old Mr. Johnson, who owned the deli, told me that someone was shaking him down for money.

While we were talking Mickey walked in and said, "What's going on, Jack?"

I replied, "Hi, Mickey. Mr. Johnson told me someone is shaking him down. The guy comes in with a hood on each week and takes a couple of hundred bucks."

Mickey looked at Mr. Johnson and said,

"Old man, you're lucky this guy don't kill you. If I were you I'd be real careful." Then Mickey walked out of the store.

Old man Johnson whispered to me, "That's him."

I said, "What?"

"That's him. I recognize his boots and voice."

"Are you sure? Mickey is one of us."

"Jack, I wouldn't lie to you. I know it's Mickey for sure. Come to think about it, he hasn't been in my store to buy anything for weeks."

"When does he usually come in for money?"

"He comes in right at closing, around midnight, usually on a Friday night. He always carries a gun."

I said, "Ok, here's the plan. It's Thursday, so tomorrow we'll set a trap. I'll be here hiding in your store at 10 pm. We have to catch him in the act. I gotta see if it's him with my own eyes. If Mickey comes in before Friday night call me."

Friday came and two of us were sitting on the floor behind the store counter. It was just me and my brother, Ron. At this point Ron was the only one I could trust. The ringing little bell, on the door, signaled someone had just entered the store.

Mr. Johnson whispered, "It's him."

Not knowing what to expect we pulled our guns. I heard a voice say, "Give me 200 bucks old man." That voice confirmed it was Mickey. Ron and I stood up from behind the counter and pointed our guns at him.

I said, "Drop the gun, Mickey." He pointed his gun at me and then at my brother.

Mickey pulled off his hood. He was waiving the gun around and said, "You guys aren't gonna shoot me."

I shouted, "Drop the gun Mickey and let's talk! Why are you doing this?"

He replied, "I got a better idea. You guys just back off. Let me go or I'm gonna shoot the old man." He pointed his gun at Mr. Johnson's head.

When Mickey did that, Ron pulled the trigger and shot him right in the heart. As he was falling he fired a round and so did I. His round went wild, but mine hit home. Our blood brother was a traitor and died on the spot.

To sum up the story, Mr. Johnson called the police. The police asked where we got the guns from. Mr. Johnson lied a little and told them they were his guns. He had them for protection behind the counter. He told them that Ron and I were there helping him clean up the store when Mickey walked in to rob him. He also told the police that Mickey shot first and we were just protecting him. It was considered a justifiable, self-defense, shooting. Ron and I never spent one night in jail.

The rest of our gang was shocked by the news. We found out that Mickey liked to gamble and was in big debt with the bookies. Two years later the gang broke up and most of us joined the military when we got out of high school. The neighborhood went to shit after that.

I should have known better than to let Park get the jump on me. I can't let Lee surprise me like that or I'll be dead for sure. Now my mind was clear and I needed to find Lee.

I put the helmet back on and tried to make sense of all the tiny lights. I saw some of them moving and it showed how far away they were in meters. I assumed these were other invisibles I was detecting. Most of the little moving red lights were 300 or more meters away. All of them were moving north towards my men. I could hear men speaking in Chinese on the radio built into the helmet.

Then I saw one tiny light that showed a distance of 75 meters and closing. I picked up my Glock and laid on the ground face first. I held the gun in my right hand underneath me. I waited as the target slowly moved closer. This has to be Lee.

After what seemed like an hour, I heard the footsteps coming up next to me. Laying face down I put my finger on the trigger. The Invisible said, "Colonel, Gwaenchanh-a? (Are you ok?)" He poked me with something.

I laid there and didn't move a muscle, but let out a little groan. I felt his hand grab my left arm to roll me over. As he rolled me over I exposed my gun and fired three rounds hitting the dork.

The soldier slowly dropped to the ground. I pulled my helmet off and hastily removed his revealing it was Lee. One of my bullets hit him in the throat. He was barely alive and gasping for air. Lee couldn't speak as blood bubbled out of his wound.

I said, "You fucking asshole." He just looked at me with his eyes wide open. I could see the hatred in his face. I put the 9 mm to his head and pulled the trigger … BAM.

I thought about what Park told me. 'The only good commie is a dead commie.' Park was right. It's too bad he didn't really believe it.

Laying next to Lee was an RPG with two rounds. There was no time to waste so I stripped off his invisible outfit and dragged him to the water to meet the same fate as Park.

I pulled out my radio and clicked the button. "Listen up! I just killed Park and Lee. They were the Commanders of Invisibles. I'm coming back with two stealth suits and an RPG."

Tommy answered, "Roger that."

I took off my stealth outfit, and picked both up, along with the RPG. I strapped the RPG rockets to my back and found my M4. The damn suits were about 35 pounds each. I was carrying about 100 pounds of gear as I humped down the road back to my men.

Arriving back at our defensive line I was dead tired. Sitting down to rest, I called Tommy over. "I got two suits. You put one on and I'll use the other. Put this RPG in the truck. Maybe we can use it."

Tommy replied, "These stealth suits could give us a big advantage."

"How's Jim Bo doing?" I asked.

"Amy took him to see the Doc. She thinks he'll need about 100 stitches."

As Tommy was putting on the stealth outfit he commented, "There's blood all over this thing."

"Sorry, I didn't have time to clean it."

"Dad, what happened out there?"

"An invisible soldier came out of nowhere and whacked me in the face. He was beating me up pretty good until I shot him. When I pulled off his helmet I was shocked to see Park. He could have killed me but he didn't. You were right. Park was a commie."

"I told you not to trust him. You almost got killed. Maybe next time you'll listen to me. You're getting too old for this shit. I hate to say it, but you're getting soft. You need to be more careful.

"The other guy was Lee, right?"

"Yeah, it was Lee."

"How'd you kill him?" Tommy asked.

"I put on Park's suit and laid on the ground pretending to be hurt. He thought I was Park and walked right up to me. I had my Glock hidden and when he rolled me over I shot him."

"What did you do with the bodies?"

"They're fish food." Tommy nodded his head in approval.

I said, "Tell me how these things work."

He put on the helmet and studied it for a while. Taking it off he told me, "The tiny red lights are the Invisibles. The heads-up display tells you their GPS location and distance.

"They also have radio communication which you can turn off with this button on the side of the helmet." Tom pointed to the button. "We should turn the radio off so they don't hear us talking. When you turn off the radio the GPS goes off." We pushed the off buttons.

"How do we sight in on these guys to shoot them?" I asked.

Pointing at the front of the helmet he said, "This is a camera. You can turn it on and off with this switch. The picture will show on the heads-up display visor. Put it on and you can see a vertical and horizontal center line on the heads-up display. That's the crosshairs."

"Yeah, I see it."

"Ok, all you do is line up the crosshairs on one of the red dots and you're looking directly at them. Then just point your weapon in that direction and fire."

I replied, "Shit that's easy. Let's go kill some dirtbags."

"Wait not so fast. Remember they can see your red dot also. When you take off the helmet or turn off the radio it turns off the GPS so they can't see you on their displays. On the other hand they can do the same thing."

"What's the plan then?"

Gunfire rang out from Mike's position in the tree nearby. Mike shouted on the radio. "I got one of them bastards! How many more are out there?"

I replied, "There are 14 more."

"I thought we were down to 12 or something. How do you figure 14?"

"Park and Lee made a total of 20. They're both dead and earlier you guys shot three. You just shot one so that leaves 14," I told him.

"Roger that 14 to go. I'm confused," Mike stated.

"Park lied to us. They never killed anyone," I told him.

I asked Tommy again, "Ok what's your plan?"

"My plan is to snipe them. We'll flank them on both sides and pick them off one by one. You take the westside and I'll take the eastside. They'll think we're Park and Lee."

The sun was just breaking the horizon and the sky was glowing red. It was a fitting sign for killing Red Chinese.

Tommy continued, "You see that big

Banyan tree on the westside?"

"Yeah, I see it."

"You make your way over there and use it for cover. Once there put on the helmet to locate the bad guys. I'll go to the other side and use that big rock for cover. It's about a 100 yards out."

"Ok, got it."

Tommy picked up his radio and clicked the button. "Heads up everyone! Jack and I are putting on stealth suits. We're gonna snipe these guys. He'll move to the big Banyan tree on the west and use it for cover. I'm going to the big boulder on the eastside. So don't shoot us. Everyone copy that?" All our men replied that the message was understood.

Tommy responded again, "One more thing. No one fire their weapon while we're out there. Hold your fire unless we radio you." One at a time they all responded affirmative.

Tom looked at me and said, "Let's see where these guys are at right now." He put on the stealth helmet and drew a picture in the dirt. He counted 14 men and marked their positions in the dirt with an X. "You have eight coming on your side of the road and I got the rest of them.

We knew their general locations. After

checking our guns and ammo supply Tom said, "Good hunting."

"Be careful. It's a jungle out there," I told him, and we both laughed. Making a joke in times of peril is a good way to let out the tension.

"Dad, when this is over, I'm taking you to Disney World." Once again we laughed and wished each other good luck.

Tommy reminded me, "Be sure to turn on the helmet radio."

We picked up our invisible helmets and started sneaking towards our sniper locations. It was hard to carry the damn helmet and also have my M4 at the ready. The suit was heavy and I couldn't move very fast. After a few minutes I was drenched in sweat and needed a drink of water. It was impossible to take a drink since my water supply was under the invisible clothes.

I thought what's the enemy doing for water? If they don't have a water supply that could work to our advantage. When the sun comes out in full force they'll slowly cook in these hot suits.

Reaching the Banyan tree I hid behind it, and put on the helmet. I noticed that one invisible was only 40 meters away. He was walking towards me. I stepped out from behind the tree, lined up the crosshairs on the display visor, and took aim. I fired five rapid rounds.

The tricky part was I didn't know if I shot him or not since I couldn't see him and the red dot was still on my screen. The only way to tell if he was still alive was to see if he moved. I waited five minutes and there was no movement so I assumed he was dead.

This whole thing was pissing me off. I could hear the soldiers speaking on the radio. I didn't know what they were saying in Chinese. I looked at the display again and this time another man was moving in the direction of the guy I had just shot. He was 15 meters away from him.

I decided to let him approach closer to the body and then shoot him. He was within five meters of the body and automatic fire pelleted the tree I was standing behind. The guy was shooting at me. My cover was already blown.

I laid down on the ground and crawled out just enough from behind the tree to get a bead on the dot. This time I sprayed the whole area with half a magazine. I waited five minutes and neither red dot showed movement so I moved forward.

I wanted to remove their helmets, which would turn off their units, and expose their heads. Then I could confirm that they were really dead. I saw there was another dot 50 meters away from the bodies. I knelt down and watched it for five minutes. It wasn't moving at all.

I stood up, creped forward, and saw a rifle flash come from the red dot that I was just watching. I heard AK47 bullets whiz by my head, so I hit the deck, and fired at the flashes. My mag ran dry, so I reloaded. I kept firing until his gun was silenced.

I could hear rifle fire coming from Tom's direction. I heard his M4 and the distinct sound of the Chinese AKs. I pushed the radio button on the side of the helmet and told Tommy, "I got three dorks." If they heard our voices, perhaps that would shake them up a little.

Tommy didn't reply for a minute. I repeated, "I got three dorks."

Tom answered, "I got three dorks too." We both laughed out loud. I figured they didn't know what the word dork meant and maybe they thought we were crazy laughing out loud over the radio.

Anyhow something worked because the red dots starting to move back towards the beach. They were swarming to the road to make faster time.

I reached the two bodies nearest me and just about fell over them. Removing the helmets I shot them in the head just to make sure they weren't faking it. I moved over to the third man and removed his hood.

His eyes were open and he looked at me and said, "Water." I gave him a bullet in the head instead of water. He would have died anyway from his wounds.

I was right, these guys the so called best of the best, didn't have any water. They were getting heat stroke which impairs your thinking and drains your physical strength. I counted the number of red dots moving quickly down the road. There were only eight of them left.

The dots started to disappear one by one. They had to be taking off the oven like clothes to move faster. I guessed they were heading for the beach to make an escape back to the gunboat.

I wanted them all dead. I took off my head gear and stripped off the suit. I was out of the hot box and could breathe again. I pulled out my camel back water hose and gulped at least a pint of warm water. Warm or not, my body needed the life-giving fluid. I looked over at the rock where Tommy was and saw he had removed his suit also.

He jogged over to me and we both sat down. Out of breath we just looked at each other trying to gain our strength and senses back by taking small sips of water. Finally he said, "Let's get them before they reach the beach." I nodded my head in agreement while sipping more water.

Tommy got on the radio. "Mike, get everyone and bring up the Hummer. The Invisibles aren't invisible anymore and they're making a run for it."

Mike responded, "Roger that. We're on the way."

A short time later Mike pulled up with the Hummer. We crammed inside and Tommy took control of the fifty caliber machine gun. The rest of us were just sitting there ready to make a fast exit.

Speeding down the road with Tom in the gun turret he yelled, "There they are, about 100 yards away. Stop!"

We all jumped out of the truck as it rolled to a stop. Tommy started firing and so did we. The soldiers started to scatter and ran for cover towards the beach.

I saw a few men fall when we fired. I wasn't positive that they were hit or just ducking to avoid being shot. We spread out and started to walk forward staying close to the Hummer in case we needed to use it for cover.

Tommy kept firing the fifty in their direction. We stopped firing because they were out of sight. Tom yelled, "You guys follow them to the beach. Mike and I will drive ahead, down the road, and circle back. We'll get them in a pincer move."

Tony, Rick, and I headed to the beach. We spread out keeping about 20 feet apart. We moved slowly searching behind every bush or tree on the sandy beach. It was a good place for an ambush, but I felt these soldiers had enough. They were trying to escape as fast as they could.

We found two of them laying on the beach, at the edge of the water. They were drinking salt water out of pure desperation. They had heat stroke and didn't know what they were doing. They had apparently dropped their weapons somewhere. As we approached them they just laid there gulping down salt water. They were totally out of their senses.

Tony and Rick walked up to them. They looked at us, held their hands up, and asked for water. Like I said earlier, we normally don't take prisoners because they need to be fed and guarded. These were dangerous men and we had no choice but to terminate them on the spot. Tony and Rick shot them both in the head. It was painless and quick. We carried the bodies out into waist deep water and pushed them into the current.

My radio hissed and Tom said, "We've got visual contact. They're getting in a small boat underneath the fishing pier."

"We're a half mile away," I told him. "Do you see a gunboat out there?"

"Negative."

"Look for a wake."

"Yeah, that makes sense." After a minute Tom replied, "I don't see any wake."

I told him, "Keep looking. Oh, by the way, we just killed two dorks. That means there should be six men in that boat."

"There are only four."

"Shit that means two are missing."

Tom answered, "We have to engage these guys now, or we could lose them. Over and Out."

I responded, "We'll search for the two that are missing and head over to your location." I could hear the 50 caliber gun firing in rapid order. He must have let loose about 300 rounds.

A short time after that Tom radioed. "Four enemy, KIA here."

We were making our way west on the beach carefully checking in the high shrubs and sea grass for the missing combatants. It was a slow process and an hour went by before we knew it.

I grabbed the radio. "Tommy have you guys seen any wakes or any kind of water movement?"

"Negative. We ain't seen shit, except for sea gulls. Maybe the gunship left when they saw their troops were losing the battle."

"We've haven't found the other two men. They could be anywhere. We're about 500 yards away from you so don't shoot us by mistake. We'll be there in 30 minutes."

We walked up to the Hummer and sat down for a break. It was almost 10 am and we were tired and hungry. We sat there and scanned the surface of the water for any unusual waves. The gulf was choppy from the wind blowing. Under these conditions it would be impossible to see any wakes.

I told Tony, "Check the other Hummer we left here. See if we can drive it." The rest of us went to the HQ office to cool off and determine our next strategy for dealing with the situation. Tommy turned the AC on high. The cold air felt great on our sweat soaked bodies. Everyone needed a rest from a long stressful night.

We were far from being out of the woods. It worried me that there are two men running around Fort Desoto who could snipe us at any minute. The invisible gunship had disappeared and it could create a lot of problems for us with its 37 mm rapid-fire cannon.

I sat down and lit up a smoke while looking

around the room. I asked, "Does anyone have any ideas how to find the missing commies?" No one replied right away.

Finally, Rick said, "Let's get a hundred men out here and search the whole island."

"I think it's too risky to bring a lot of men out here. It'll give them a lot of targets to shoot at. Besides they can't get off the island without a boat."

Mike said, "See if we can get a drone from Captain Sessions."

I, nodded in agreement. "That's a good idea. Sessions will need to send drones anyway to look for that gunboat. If the drone spots the Reds we'll set a trap."

Just then Tony walked in and said, "The Hummer runs and is somewhat drivable, but it needs a new tire and some body work. I found an MK 153 we left inside and some ammo."

I said, "Thanks for the report. We were just discussing how to trap the two commies out here. Do you have any proposals?"

"They need food and water to survive. If I was them I'd scout out the base for water. We all know there's food and water stored here. Sooner or later they'll find them."

"Good points," I told him. "We need to

stake out the storehouse."

The Rangers had built a storehouse for food and water. It contains six months supply for 500 people. It is located near the HQ building in a clearing close to the chow hall. We can view this location from several look-out spots. The best one is on top of the fort wall. From there we can see the entire perimeter.

Tommy butted in, "They'll probably hunker down during the day and move at night. Without food or water they'll have to surrender sooner or later."

Rick commented, "We need to pick up all those invisible suits so they don't get a hold of them."

"I forgot about that," I replied. "Let's go find them now. While y'all look for the suits I'll get four Amazons and come back here for guard duty. First let me call Sessions."

I pulled out my cell and pushed Sessions number. He answered, "Hello, Sessions here." I put the phone on speaker mode.

"Captain, it's Jack. We have a situation here. Chinese soldiers invaded the fort using stealth-suit technology. We terminated all the men except for two. They're hiding out somewhere around the fort. They also have an invisible gunboat. The gunboat has vanished."

Sessions replied, "It sounds like you been busy. We knew they had stealth technology, but have never seen it. We weren't aware they had a stealth gunboat. How can I help you?"

"We need you to fly a drone over the fort area tonight using infrared cameras to locate the two missing men. Set up a direct video feed to my phone showing their location. In addition, we should eliminate the threat of the gunboat. Maybe you can have a drone knock it out."

"Ok, I'll send up two drones at dusk. By the way did you capture any of the stealth outfits?"

"Yes, we'll hold them for you."

"Alright, a drone will be on the way. Do you want the drone to fire on the soldiers?"

"Negative. Just advise their location because some of my men will be out there searching for them also. I don't want them shot by mistake."

"Roger that. I'll send a missile drone to eliminate the stealth boat. Where was its last location?"

"It was in the channel between Egmont Island and Fort Desoto. I assume it sailed out into the Gulf."

"Understood. We'll find it and will advise

you when it's destroyed."

"Roger that, Captain. That's all for now."

"Good hunting."

Rick said, "Let's get going and find those stealth outfits."

Tommy and Mike stayed behind to guard the storehouse. Rick drove me to Shark Channel Bridge and dropped me off to meet with the Amazons. He returned to the battle ground to help find the stealth uniforms. I advised him to collect the outfits and take them to our gun vault for security reasons. I didn't want anyone to get their hands on them.

I approached the Amazons who were standing guard on the bridge. They were all there except for Amy who was taking care of Jim's injury. I climbed up into the bed of the closest pickup truck and the women warriors all gathered around me.

I shouted, "We've killed all the invaders except for two. Two of them are still loose in Fort Desoto. I need four volunteers for guard duty at the fort. We have to protect the warehouse and if possible capture these men."

Before I could finish my speech I noticed that Trini, Maggie, Lisa, and Wanda, raised their hands. Others were also waving their hands in the air. I looked around the group and said, "Thank you all for volunteering. I want you to know that this is a dangerous assignment. I only need four people."

I needed the best Amazons for this assignment. Trying not to look selective, I peered around and slowly picked out Maggie, Lisa, Trini, and Wanda. Then I commented, "Half of you to stay on guard duty here. The rest of you take a break and get some rest. We'll do four hour shifts until all the commies are found."

I asked Wanda, "How's your Chinese?"

"It's still pretty good."

"Great, I need you to translate a message to the Chinese soldiers."

I selected the best Amazon Warriors. I needed warriors who had experience. I wanted warriors who had actually killed someone. I wanted a warrior who would not hesitate to kill the commies. I wanted warriors that I could trust.

Wanda had been in combat, but she had never actually killed anyone. She is physically tough and a good soldier. She obeys orders to the letter. The reason I chose her was because she is Chinese-American. Wanda can speak and read Chinese. Her father came here 30 years ago and opened a Chinese restaurant. Wanda, a good-looking single woman, also works in the mess hall with Steve adding a little Chinese flair to our food. She's in great shape and knows Kung Fu.

My general plan was to drive slowly around the fort and let Wanda use a megaphone. She would speak in Chinese and tell the men to surrender. If they surrender we'd provide them food and water.

I brought along Maggie, Trini, and Lisa, because they would relish the chance to kill our enemies. They are the best women warriors I have. You can trust them with your life.

Maggie is methodical and thinks before acting. She is also my most trusted woman warrior. I've seen her in action. I'll never forget when she chopped off a gang leader's head. Maggie keeps her cool and is fearless.

Lisa is the youngest and the strongest Amazon. She knows how to use any weapon and is deadly with a knife. Rico had trained her to be one of the best. I knew in a bind she could take care of herself.

Trini is just a natural born killer. She likes killing bad guys. She has no fear of anything. She has speed and the fastest reflexes I've ever seen. I often worry about her because she's so blood-thirsty.

I radioed Amy and told her what I was

doing. She advised me Jim was doing fine but he'd be out of commission for a few days. Amy told me she'd be back on duty in an hour.

I told Wanda to find the hand-held megaphone which was at the old bank building. While she was gone I had a meeting with my warriors and told them, "If these guys surrender we'll put them in the cell block and question them one at a time. After that we have no use for them."

Trini asked, "Do you mean we … let them try and escape?" Trini giggled and gave me an evil smile while rubbing her hands together. Lisa and Maggie looked at her and shook their heads.

"Yes, they'll try to escape while you're guarding them," I told her.

Trini replied, "Goodie."

"Maggie said, "Trini, you're sick."

"I know that."

I butted in, "Anyway I want the three of you to make sure they're terminated. Wanda is along because she can speak Chinese. Once we capture these guys and interrogate them she'll go back to Tocabaga. Y'all will stay on guard duty with me."

Maggie asked, "What if they don't surrender?"

"If they don't surrender then we shoot them on sight. Anymore questions?" No one replied as Wanda came walking up with the megaphone.

I said, "Mount up. We gotta go."

I was driving the 4 door pickup truck as we went to the fort. All of the Amazons were in the pickup bed except for Maggie. Wanda was using the megaphone and was yelling for them to surrender as we drove down the road. Trini and Lisa were watching our backs from the pickup bed.

I told Maggie, "We're gonna slowly drive from one end of the fort to the other. Then we'll go back to the storehouse and set up a look-out post on the fort wall. Keep your eyes open."

Maggie nodded her head. "Don't worry, I will."

End-to-end the fort road is about four miles long. The road runs east-west and makes a dog leg turn at Fort Desoto HQ and then runs north-south.

Wanda was speaking Chinese into the megaphone. "Drop your weapons and surrender now. If you surrender we will provide you food and water. Your Commander, Colonel Park, is dead. Surrender now!" She repeated this message every few minutes.

My guess was that the enemy soldiers were

somewhere around the Fort HQ already. They were somewhere close to our warehouse. I knew they badly needed water.

We completed the loop on the fort road, but the commies didn't come out to surrender. I pulled up to the HQ building and we dismounted. I told Tom and Mike to take a break and help find the stealth clothes. They drove off in the damaged Hummer.

I told Trini and Lisa, "You'll provide security here at the HQ and the warehouse. Patrol around the buildings and watch your backs. Stay alert and if you hear or see anything, radio me."

They answered, "Yes sir." Trini smiled and giggled. It pissed me off she wasn't taking this dangerous situation seriously.

I warned them again, "Stay alert, this is no joke. These guys are dangerous and will kill you if they can. Maggie and Wanda you're with me on top of the bunker wall. From there we can see anyone approaching the warehouse. Wanda you keep repeating the message."

Reaching the top of the 40-foot high bunker wall, I said, "Maggie, you watch the warehouse. Wanda, start using that megaphone and I'll watch our backsides."

I looked at the sky and then my watch. It

had been a long day. Soon it would be dark again. I clicked my radio. "Mike, did you guys find all the stealth suits?"

"All but one," he answered.

"Ok, tell the men to keep looking."

"Roger that. Have you seen the two enemy combatants yet?"

"Negative."

"It'll be getting dark soon. Do you have any orders for us?" I didn't respond right away because I was planning what to do when it gets dark.

"Boss, are you still there?"

"Yeah, I'm thinking what to do when it gets dark and we still haven't caught these guys. You got any suggestions?"

"We have the stealth clothes so why not use them?" Mike said.

"Good idea. How would you do that?"

"We put them on and stake out our buildings. I'll bring a couple over right now."

"It's almost dark, so bring them here ASAP. Mike, tell Tommy to come along and bring his 308 sniper rifle."

"Roger that. We'll be there as soon as I find

him."

"Over."

I looked at Maggie and asked, "You seen anything?"

"Nothing at all."

"Can you see Trini and Lisa."

"Not right now. They're on the other side of the building."

Then I heard a shot come from the storehouse area. I said, "What the fuck!" The shot I heard definitely came from an M4. The Chinese use AK47s.

I picked up the radio. "Lisa, Trini, come in! What's going on?"

"Trini, Lisa, come in!" There was no response.

Maggie and Wanda looked at me with worried faces. "Girls, make sure your weapons are cocked and locked. We're going down there. Follow me and stay alert."

We slowly slid down the side of the thick weed-covered wall. Reaching ground level I took the point with Wanda in the rear providing security.

We passed by the front of the HQ building. I looked at the door and tried to open it. It was secure showing no apparent break in. There's a 300-foot space between the HQ building and the warehouse.

The warehouse contains food, water, and weapons in a secure vault. The building itself is all metal with six windows. The entire thing is bullet proof. Breaking into this building is pretty much impossible. Once the Reds figured that out they would look for a softer target to obtain food and water.

There are three doors on the building. The north side has a single door. The south side has a double door and an overhead door. We approached the south side first because we could see it was all clear from the HQ building.

Arriving at the south side I could see the doors were secure and hadn't been disturbed. I said, "Wanda you stay here and provide security. If anyone comes around the corner blast them. Maggie you're with me. We're gonna circle around the building."

Reaching the first corner I pulled out a small mirror and held it out to peek around the corner. It was clear so we rapidly moved up to the next corner which would provide us a view of the north side which we couldn't see from on top of the wall.

Holding my mirror out I saw two bodies on the ground. I peeked my head out and scanned the area as far as I could see. Peering out to the edge of dense jungle, 100 yards away, I saw no one.

I ducked back and told Maggie. "Trini and Lisa are down. I didn't see anyone else. We're going to move them inside the warehouse. You provide cover while I drag them inside."

"Ok," Maggie replied.

"Let's make this fast."

We darted out from around the corner and trotted cautiously up to the first body which was laying right in front of the door. It was Trini laying in a pool of blood with her machete in her hand. I slung my weapon and unlocked the door. Picking her up, I saw the blood running from her mouth and neck. I laid her down on the floor and went out to pick up Lisa.

Maggie was on one knee scanning around and said, "We got company. A truck is coming this way."

"That's Tom and Mike."

I picked up Lisa and she was semi-conscious. While putting her on the floor she asked, "What ... happened?"

I noticed right away that both their guns were missing along with their water supplies, tactical vests, ammo, and any food they may have had.

I gave Lisa a drink of water and told her, "Lie still, while I check Trini."

I moved over to Trini and shined my flashlight on her face and clothes. She had lost a lot of blood. Her color wasn't good. I ripped opened her blood soaked shirt to look for wounds. She had been shot in the lower neck. I felt for a pulse, but there was none. She was gone for sure. There was nothing I could do.

Bowing my head, I prayed for Trini, "Dear Lord, please accept this brave warrior into your kingdom." I gently pushed her eyes closed and folded her hands across her chest. Finding a tarp nearby, I covered her body.

Lisa heard me and asked, "What did you say?"

"Trini is gone."

These dirty bastards killed Trini one of our best warriors. She was a little wild, but you could always count on her. I'll get these guys and they'll pay for this. Justice will be served. An eye for an eye is my motto.

Lisa tried to get up, but her neck was injured and she couldn't move. She cried, "Why … why did she have to die!" Lisa started to sob.

I bent over Lisa and checked her neck. The bad guys beat her up pretty good. Looking at her closer she had a couple of big welts on her face. I felt the back of her head and there was a large lump oozing blood.

I asked her, "Can you remember what happen?"

"No. I didn't see anything."

"Do you know me?"

"Of course, you're Rico, my boy friend."

"No, I'm Jack … Jack Gunn."

Lisa looked at me kinda funny, and said, "Yeah, that's what I said."

"Lisa don't move. Your neck is sprained and you have a bad concussion. Doc needs to check you out."

Maggie peeked in the door and asked, "How are they doing?"

"Not good. Lisa has a bad concussion and her neck is severely sprained. I'm sorry to say, Trini is gone." I walked to the front door to unlock it for Wanda. "Wanda, guard this door from the inside. Maggie keep your eyes open over there."

In an angry tone Maggie growled, "I wanna kill these guys myself." I didn't say a word back to her. I knew if she had the chance Maggie would make them suffer.

A few minutes later Mike and Tommy pulled up in front of the building. I met them at the door. Tommy could tell something was wrong by the expression on my face. "What happened?"

"They killed Trini and Lisa is hurt pretty bad. No one saw what happened."

"Shit, how'd they kill Trini?" Tom asked.

"They shot her with her own gun, as far as I can tell."

Mike and Tom pulled back the tarp and both gazed at her body. After a minute they covered her up.

Mike spoke up, "That's the third Amazon killed in the line of duty."

Maggie told us, "I was on guard. I was watching their backs from the wall and I didn't see anyone. I let them down."

I asked Mike, "Did you find that missing stealth outfit?"

"Negative," Mike replied.

"That's it, the guy had on a stealth suit. That's how they did this."

"That makes a lot of sense," Tommy said.

"Maggie get the truck and take Lisa and Trini to Doc Scott's office."

While they went for the pickup we carefully strapped Lisa to a stretcher. I didn't want to tell her that her neck maybe fractured. We slid Trini into a body bag and were all silent as Mike zipped it closed. Gently we picked up the body and loaded it into the bed of the pickup.

I advised the girls to get to the Doc as fast as possible and to get some rest after that. The warriors drove away just as the sun was setting. We watched them until they were out of sight.

Mike tossed me an invisible suit and said, "Let's get these bastards."

My phone rang so I answered it. "Mr. Gunn, this is Sergeant Smith at SOCOM. Your drone is overhead now and here's the live feed."

I held my phone out for Mike and Tommy to see.

The drone was directly overhead and we could see the warehouse and other buildings. It was flying an east-west pattern over the island. The video was being shown in infrared. If the commies were here we'd find them now.

Tommy suggested, "Let me take the phone and go to the top of the wall. Maybe I can get a shot from up there. You guys stay here and I'll radio you their location."

"Ok, that sounds good." I told him.

Looking at Tom, Mike replied, "If you can't take them out then we'll move in using the invisible suits."

I gave Tom the phone and he took off in a flash. With his 308, and FLIR scope, he could reach out 800 yards and kill these dorks. Mike and I slipped into the invisible units.

Pulling the helmet over my head I saw one red light. It was north of us, in the woods, about 500 meters away. Mike saw it also and said, "Well that confirms they got one suit."

I clicked my radio and told Tommy we found one of them using the invisible suit and gave him a general location to search. Tommy advised back, "I've redirected the drone to that area."

I replied, "We're on the way there now."

Mike and I were heading to the location to intercept the enemy. I heard Tommy on my radio and we stopped. "The drone isn't picking you up. I can see one man with my FLIR."

"Yeah, that makes sense because you can't see the invisible's heat signature. That means the drone is picking up the guy that doesn't have on stealth clothes."

Tommy responded, "I got that guy on my scope. I'm taking him out."

I answered, "Take the ass-hole out."

A minute later we heard the echo of his 308 ring through the jungle. Then we heard it again. A few seconds later it repeated one more time.

Tommy radioed, "The target is down."

"Good shooting," I said.

Mike tapped me on the arm indicating for me to put on my helmet. I placed it on my head and saw the red light coming for us. He was 300 meters away and heading in our direction.

Mike said, "I suggest we do a 'V' shaped ambush."

Using a 'V' shaped ambush we're the top of the V. Where the lines meet, at the bottom of the V, is the target zone. We picked out a big tree a 100 yards out to be our target zone. When the enemy is near that point we take him out.

Mike moved 50 yards to the right and I moved 50 yards to the left. We aimed our lasers on the tree. I pulled out my radio to advise Tommy what we were doing.

I asked him, "Can you see Mike's laser on a

tree?"

"Negative. Where is it again?" I gave him more detailed directions where to look.

"I see the dot."

"Ok, keep looking in that direction. When you see our lasers paint the target, open fire."

"Roger that."

Mike and I were prone watching the tiny red spot on the heads up display come closer and closer. Suddenly he stopped moving. He was probably wondering why we weren't moving. He could see we were waiting for him. He knew it was a trap.

How stupid I was; forgetting that he could see us as well. *What the hell was I thinking?* I wasn't thinking straight. My brain was dwelling on the fact that Trini was dead and I wanted vengeance. I wanted an eye for an eye. No, I wanted more than an eye. I wanted to make this scumbag suffer. I wanted to hurt him really bad. I wanted to give him more than just a bullet.

Clearing my train of thought, I took off my helmet and clicked the radio. "Mike, come in."

A moment later Mike replied, "I'm here."

"These suits are for shit. The guy can see us and knows we're setting a trap."

"Yep, it appears he knows we're waiting for him."

"Tommy, you on the line?"

"Yes, go ahead."

"Ok, listen up. I'm taking off this thing. I am gonna stalk him using Mike to guide me to him. Mike you move around and play hide and seek with him while I zero in on his location. Take your helmet off every now and then to disappear. Radio me his position and I'll move straight towards him."

I stripped off the hot invisible suit.

"Tommy, you keep scanning the woods for him. If you get a shot take it, but make sure you're shooting him and not me. Once you paint the target radio me."

Tommy replied, "I'll know if it's you because my FLIR will show your heat signature. He won't show one."

"That's a good point, as long as he doesn't take off his suit."

"That's right."

"Any other comments or questions?" I asked.

Both replied, "Negative."

"Ok, let's do this. Over."

I preceded straight forward deeper into the jungle. It was dark now and I hate moving through the bush in the dark. It's just plain scary. You risk snake bites, spider bites, and now even wild pigs could attack you.

Crouching low, trying not to make any noise, I had moved about 30 yards. There was a slight breeze blowing which moved the leaves and small tree branches. I knelt down on one knee and held there for a minute listening for any type of noise.

I had cleared my mind now. I just wanted this over with. I wanted to be the one to put a bullet in this dork's head. Where is this guy, I wondered? Ten minutes went by with no communication from Mike.

I heard a slight buzzing overhead. It was the drone making a pass. My radio hissed and Tom came on. "I confirm one dead commie."

I whispered back, "Roger."

In the woods we have a lot of old big pine trees. I know it seems weird pine trees growing in a tropical climate but certain species do. There's the Slash Pine and the Sand Pine Tree that can reach 60 feet high and grow 2-3 feet in diameter. When the wind blows through the tops it makes a whistling sound. The trees grow in groups of five to ten.

I was kneeling at the foot of one of these trees, in a bed of thick pine needles sprinkled with pine cones. It smelled good and reminded me of Christmas time in the old days.

I heard a noise to my right and scoped it out. It was only a raccoon searching for food. I shined my laser around the area just to be sure. The woods are dense and thick making it almost impossible to walk without making any noise. Sooner or later I would hear the killer and get a bead on him.

"Jack, where are you at?" Mike asked over the radio.

Softly I replied, "At the foot of the big pine tree. I'm at the point of the 'V' for the ambush location."

"The target is about 50 meters directly to your right."

"Roger that."

I raised my M4 and started to scan the area with my laser. The thick foliage intercepted the beam making it impossible to see 50 meters. I needed to move closer to get a clean shot.

"Mike, is he still there?" I asked.

"Yeah, he's not moving."

I rose up in a low crouch and started to make my way towards the target. It was slow going picking my way through the dense bushes. If I made any noise it could get me killed. It was taking me five minutes to take ten steps.

After 30 minutes I called Mike, "Is he still there?"

"Affirmative. He hasn't moved."

I scanned the area with my laser. After a couple of minutes I saw him. I picked up the large red dot out of the bushes. I was sure it was the invisible man. I aimed my rifle and flicked off the safety.

Suddenly my radio came on and Tommy said, "I'm picking up two heat signatures. He's got a bead on you. Get out of there now!"

I dropped and rolled just as a bullet whizzed by striking the leaves near my arm. I quickly crawled on my hands and knees as more bullets zoomed overhead.

That was too close for comfort. My heart was pounding. The killer had taken off the suit and used it for bait. It was a trap. This guy was smart, but not that smart. He didn't know that Tommy was on the wall watching him and that we had a drone.

I crawled to another pine tree about 20 feet away. He had one of our M4's which has a FLIR scope so he could see my body heat.

I muttered softly into my radio, "Tommy, if you got a shot take it."

"Negative. I don't have a clear shot."

Mike came on, "I'm taking off my suit also. I'll circle around behind him."

I replied, "Negative. Stay put for now."

I couldn't talk anymore because he was coming. I turned off my radio. I slid under some 3 foot high ferns, rolled on my back, and covered most of my body with pine needles. Pine needles are an excellent heat insulator. I smeared dirt all over my face trying to reduce my heat signature.

I looked through my FLIR scope but couldn't see him. Maybe he was behind me. Maybe he was in front of me. Laying on my back I couldn't get a good view. I stopped breathing and tried to listen more intently. The only thing I heard was my heart beating. I laid my M4 on the ground next to me and drew my Glock. Laying on my back it would be easier for me to use my pistol if he was within range.

This guy was good. He knew how to sneak and peak. He must be one of their best snipers. I heard him, a twig snapped, over to my right. I turned my head to look, but didn't see a thing. I couldn't hear him walking any more. He must have stopped and is scanning around with the scope looking for me.

For a few minutes I only heard the wind whistling in the pine trees. I didn't move a muscle and was breathing very shallow. I held my breath every few seconds.

Then I heard a soft crunch; the sound of steps on soft pine needles. They were slow uneven steps that stopped and paused after one or two strides. He was coming closer because each step was getting louder. He had to be right next to me.

Laying on my back I saw the ferns move above my head and he stepped forward. The killer was standing right next to my legs. One more stride and he'd be stepping on me.

Looking into his rifle scope, he didn't see me. He had no idea I was on the ground right next to him hidden under the ferns. I slowly raised my gun and aimed at him. All of a sudden he pushed aside a fern leaf, looked down, and spotted me.

I had a clear shot and before he could move another muscle I pulled the trigger … BAM … BAM, BAM. I fired three rounds, one round to the head and two to the body. He fell across my legs hitting the ground in a thud.

I kicked him off of my legs and quickly stood up. Pointing the Glock at the back of his head I fired one more round just to make sure he was dead. I sat down, on his back, and lit up a smoke. After taking a deep drag I blew out a smoke ring with a sense of relief and took a drink of water.

I looked at the dead body and said, "An eye for an eye, you dirty commie." It made me feel good, real good, knowing I had terminated Trini's killer. I put my smoke out by crushing it into his brain bucket. It made a good ash-tray. The wet blood snuffed out the butt right away.

My adrenaline rush was gone and so was all my energy. I turned my radio on and advised Mike and Tom. "The killer is dead. I'm dragging his body out now."

Tommy said, "I was a little worried about you."

Mike answered, "Good job, old man."

Tommy replied, "Let's just leave the bodies in the jungle for the pigs to eat."

I commented, "Now, that's a good idea. I didn't wanna drag his dead ass around anyway."

I dropped the body and headed back to the warehouse. It was a fit ending for the commies letting the pigs eat them.

Arriving back at the warehouse the three of us shook hands and gave thanks to God for protecting us from evil. After that I said, "I need a drink."

Mike replied, "I'll drive, let's go."

Riding back to the bar, which we call 'The Green Room,' we stopped at Shark Channel Bridge. We informed the Amazons the enemy had been terminated.

Amy commented, "Yeah, we've been listening to the radio chatter and figured you guys got them. Dad, you killed the guy that got Trini?"

"Yep, I killed one of the bastards and Tommy the other."

"How did you kill them?" Maggie asked.

"I used a triple tap. Then I gave him one more in the head to make sure he was dead. Tommy took the other guy out with his 308. We left the bodies in the woods for pigs to eat. How's Lisa doing?"

Maggie replied, "Doc says she needs to wear a neck brace for a few days but nothing is broken. She'll be ok."

"She was really lucky," Amy commented.

I advised them, "You can go back to normal guard duty here on the bridge. We're gonna get a drink or two and then head home. Good job warriors. Oh, by the way Trini and Lisa's rifles are in our truck."

At the Green Room everyone wanted to know all the details. I just wanted a drink and didn't want to think about it. The more you talk about it the worst your nightmares become. So I try to wipe it out of my mind. I don't like telling stories about what I did.

Mike and Tommy feel the same way so they blew the people off and told them we'll talk about it later. We just wanted to have a drink in peace and go home.

Mike and I had one drink and then went over to see Lisa at the medical office.

Lisa said, "Boy, I'm happy to see you guys."

Doc Scott said, "Don't stay to long she needs a lot of rest."

"How do you feel Lisa?" I asked.

"Not bad, but I still don't remember what happened. Did you kill the commies?"

Mike said, "Yeah we got them all. Jack killed the one that got Trini."

I notice that Mike reached out and touched Lisa's hand. Observing that I told them, "Well, I'll see you both tomorrow. I gotta get some sleep."

Lisa responded, "Bye, Jack, and thanks."

I thought it would be great if Mike and Lisa

hooked up. I think they're a match for each other.

I went back to the bar and downed three double shots. Tommy drove us home. I was pretty drunk because I was tired and basically had nothing to eat all day. I hadn't had more than two hours sleep in two days.

It was 10 pm when we walked in the house and we were greeted by our wives and kids. I had some fruit with a hard-boiled egg and then took a shower. The shower made me feel a lot better.

I fell onto the bed exhausted. My wife started to give me a back rub. It felt great and helped me relax those sore muscles. I advised her that the Red Chinese were stopped for the time being and that Park was dead. I also gave her the bad news that Trini was killed.

She didn't say a word about Trini, but told me. "I'm proud of you, but you take too many risks."

That's all I remember before passing out from exhaustion.

JULY 11, 2025

The kids were yelling, "Wake up Grandpa!" My grandchildren were in the room poking me to wake up. I started to laugh because it tickled. I jumped out of bed, growled like a bear, and they ran downstairs screaming.

I love all my grandkids, Johnny, Jimmy, Shanda, Billy, Rosie, Peter, and Kendra. I think that's all of them. They have, more or less, a normal life free of worry and violence here on Tocabaga. The only one to leave the island recently was Johnny, when Federal agents kidnapped us both.

That reminded me I need to call Rico and tell him about the Chinese invasion. I also promised Rico I would come over and help him out. Looking at the clock it was almost noon.

I gotta call Captain Sessions and advise him that we stopped the Reds from gaining a foot hold. I wondered if they found the invisible gunboat?

While taking a shower I found a tick in my arm. I could see it, but needed someone to remove it. If you don't remove a tick it can cause a fever and infection. My muscles were sore from two days of being on the go. My knees were cracking with each step. They just plain hurt each time I stood up.

I had black and blue marks all over my face and body. Park gave me two black eyes after bashing me in the face. There was a gash on my forehead from hitting it on the inside of the Hummer. I cleaned the gash with peroxide and alcohol. Then I applied some antibiotic cream.

I was brushing my teeth and found a couple of loose front teeth. *I'll go to Doc Scott and have him put some surgical super glue around my gums to hold them tight until they heal. If they keep wiggling around I might lose them.* I shaved my head and trimmed my goatee.

After putting on a tee shirt and jeans, I went down to the kitchen for some chow. Hemmi said, "You look like a walking zombie. Sit down. I made some fried eggs and chicken."

I said, "Before I eat get some tweezers and pull this tick out of my arm."

"Let me see it." Hemmi looked at it and went to the cabinet for the medical kit.

I pulled out a chair and sat down exposing the back of my arm. As she picked up the tweezers I told her, "Grab it close to the skin. Make sure you get the head out."

We have a lot of experience removing ticks. The dirty little blood suckers are all over the place. That's one reason why I shave my head. We check each other for ticks every week.

I could feel Hemmi pulling on the tick. She was slowly pulling the bug out from under my skin. Hemmi commented, "I got the bastard. It's a big one." She held it up, close to my face, showing me the half inch long blood sucker.

"Flush it down the toilet," I told her.

Hemmi came back and poured me a cup of hot java. I asked, "Where did everyone go?"

"Give me your arm. I'll put some alcohol on it to kill the germs." While cleaning the tick wound she said, "The kids are outside playing. The men are on guard duty and doing whatever it is they do."

She finished cleaning my wound and told me. "Jim is able to hobble around and went down to the main bridge. Amy and Tommy are arranging for Trini's funeral service to be held tomorrow."

"Yeah, it's a damn shame that Trini got killed. Everyone will miss her. She was a great warrior. I feel somewhat responsible for her death."

"Jack, you can't protect everybody."

I finished eating, grabbed another cup of coffee, and went out on the patio for a smoke. Hemmi followed me out and asked, "Are we safe from a Chinese invasion for the time being?"

"Yeah, for now, but I fear they'll be back."

"I couldn't believe that Park tried to kill you. He was so friendly to us and the kids."

"Park had me fooled, but not Tommy. I should have killed him sooner."

"Did he give you those black eyes?"

I nodded my head and asked, "Could you please get me two aspirins? My whole body hurts."

Hemmi brought me the aspirins and a shot of JD. I downed both and said, "Thanks honey."

"You need to take it easy today. I don't want you to do anything but relax all day. You got that," she ordered.

"Don't worry, I will."

"Why do you have to take all the risks? You have over a hundred men. Let some of them take a risk. The Gunn family does enough for this island."

"Look honey, I was elected Head of Security. I have to lead by example. I wouldn't ask anyone to do something that I wouldn't do. You have to lead from the front not the rear. What I do is for the Gunn family and the whole island."

"Yeah, I guess you're right."

"So far a number of our people have been killed in the line of duty. Everyone here chips in and takes their chances on the front line. Everyone here pitches in and works hard for Tocabaga. I'm just doing my fair share."

"If you ask me you're doing more than your fair share."

"Ok, look at it this way. Who else would you want to head up security?"

"No one, I guess. I just don't want a dead husband."

I walked over, bent down, and gave her a kiss on the cheek. Holding her face gently in my hands, I said, "Don't worry honey. I'm always careful out there."

"I know you are, but your no spring chicken anymore."

"No, but you're still a TYC." We both laughed as I gave her a big hug.

She worries every time I go into combat.

She has to let her feelings out. She has to let her stress out. I can understand how she feels. Hemmi worries about me and her family. She needs to keep busy so there's no time to worry.

I asked, "What are you doing today?"

"I was going to take Shanda and Kendra to farming school at 3 pm."

"Are the boys going also?"

"No, they don't like farming."

"I got an idea. Why don't we all go to farming school? I think the boys should learn how to farm."

The children on Tocabaga haven't been to school for a few days due to the commie invasion. On Tocabaga we have about 25 kids under the age of 16. Every day, for three hours, they learn farming, hunting, cooking, shooting, and fishing. They also attend classes at the church for three hours to learn history, math, reading, computers, and the Constitution. We teach our kids U.S. history and how the United States was in the past. We teach them how the country came to be this way.

Young men and women over the age of 16 are given a choice of what trade they would like to be in. If they choose security then they undergo a very rigorous training process. Whatever they choose each one is assigned a mentor to be with them for the next two years. Most of the time, one of their parents is their mentor. By the time they reach adulthood our kids are well-educated and trained how to survive. They know how to protect themselves from evil.

I went outside to find Johnny and Jimmy. I called their names and they came running right away. They both jumped up into my arms and I hugged them.

Johnny said, "Grandpa, how'd you get those black eyes?"

Jimmy repeated, "Yeah, how'd that happen?"

I put the boys down and I thought for a minute before replying. I knelt down on one knee and said, "Well boys. You know there are bad men in this world. I had a fight with one of them and got these black eyes."

Johnny asked, "Does it hurt?"

Johnny and Jimmy saw their real parents killed by al-Qaida. Johnny saved his little brother and Captain Sessions from certain death by hiding them until it was safe.

"It hurts a little," I said.

"Did you kill the bad guy?" Johnny asked.

It's sad when a little ten-year-old kid has to ask his Grandpa such a question. How do you answer that? You can only tell the truth.

"Yes, I had to kill him because he was trying to kill me. You remember, Mr. Park? Well, he was the bad guy."

"You had to kill Mr. Park?" Johnny asked.

"Yes, he turned out to be a communist and tried to kill me."

Jimmy asked, "What's a communist?"

"A communist is a person who believes that the government should own everything. They want to control everything in your life. They want to tell everyone what to do. Mr. Park lied to me and he was a communist who wanted to control Tocabaga."

The kids were speechless and just looked at me.

"Kids, you never know who is telling the truth. You never know who you can trust. Let that be a lesson."

"I want be a fighter like you, Grandpa. When I get older I'll protect you from the bad men," Johnny said.

"Me too," Jimmy replied.

It broke my heart to hear them say that. I hate to think that they will grow up and still be fighting for freedom. It means I have to train my boys as best as I can. Tommy and I will have to start their training soon. It's time they learn how to shoot. The sooner you start shooting the better you become as you get older. On the other hand there's a lot of other things they need to learn. Just thinking about it is over whelming. We need to go step by step. I'll try to cram everything I know into their little brains. The children are the future. Without them we have none.

I told them, "I know you'll protect me. Now, let's go to the farm. You need to learn how to grow food."

I called out for Shanda and Kendra and they came running. I asked, "What were you girls doing?"

Kendra answered, "We were on the seawall watching the fish."

"I told you not to go on the seawall unless an adult is with you. If you fall in the sharks will eat you."

Shanda said, "Uncle Ron was with us."

Just then Ron walked around the corner.

Ron commented, "Bro, you look like crap."

"Thanks, Bro. I feel like crap. We're going to the farm. You wanna come along?"

"No, thanks. I have guard duty tonight. See you later."

Ron, my younger brother, is a man of few words. He would never ask me what happened out in the bush. Ron is a man of action. He's strong and has endless energy. I don't where he gets it from since he's over weight and out of shape. When I have to leave the compound Ron stays behind most of the time to protect the family.

I went to the gun safe and pulled out my Glock and M4. I also picked up Hemmi's pistol with a shoulder hostler. We don't go far from home without our guns.

Hemmi's gun of choice is a Ruger 22 caliber target pistol with a red dot scope. It's loaded with hollow points and each mag holds ten rounds. She's a deadly shot with this weapon and can place all ten rounds in a two inch target at 50 yards.

We climbed into the Humvee and started for the farm. I stopped at Doc's office for a minute to see Lisa. Everyone climbed out of the truck and walked into the office. Mike was there with Lisa. She was sitting in a chair with a neck brace on.

I asked, "How you doing?"

Lisa said, "Hi everyone. Thanks for coming to see me. I'm doing ok. Doc told me I could go home today but not to do anything strenuous. He wants me to stay home for another three days. After that I can take off this stupid brace."

Mike looked at me and said, "You look worse than Lisa."

"Very funny," I told him. "What's up?"

"I'm helping Lisa out until she's better."

"Yeah, I can see that." We all laughed at that comment.

The kids looked at her and Johnny asked, "What's wrong with you?"

"A commie hit me in the head when I was on guard duty."

Johnny peered up at me and asked, "Grandpa, are there anymore commies around here?"

"No, not now Johnny."

"When I'm big I promised to protect Grandpa. I'll protect you too Lisa," Johnny told her.

"Hey, me too," Jimmy responded.

Shanda said, "You're brave, Lisa. I wanna

be strong and brave like you."

"Yeah, I wanna be a warrior also," Kendra advised. "Mom said we could be Amazon Warriors."

Hemmi jumped in, "Ok, kids we gotta go. Lisa needs her rest." Everyone gave their goodbyes and we went to the farm.

The farm is located on the same island as Fort Desoto. As a matter of fact some of the fighting took place in our fields. There's a low voltage three-foot-high fence running around the small farm to keep the pigs and other critters out. The fence is powered by solar panels which also charge a bank of batteries.

Twenty people were hoeing the fields and removing weeds. Another group was picking vegetables and fruit from the trees. Everything would be loaded into baskets and taken to the storage area which Steve is in charge of. Anyone can take freshly picked food home to enjoy.

I told Hemmi, "You go ahead and take the kids around and teach them about the different plants. I gotta call Sessions and Rico. I'll be right back. Oh, by the way, watch out for snakes."

I jumped in the truck and drove to the HQ. I wanted to look around to make sure everything was in order and that no guns were lying around. I found a big rock, where Lisa had been lying, which was probably used to whack her. As near as I can figure the guy hit Lisa, knocking her out and jumped Trini before she knew what happened. He managed to overpower her, taking her gun, and shot her. Trini did manage to draw her machete before getting killed. The stealth uniform made it possible for him to sneak up on them and escape without being seen.

SUMMARY OF PHONE CALL TO CAPTAIN SESSIONS

I called Sessions and told him that everything was under control here and that the fort was secure. We had stopped the Reds from gaining a foot-hold in our area. However, it cost us several injuries and the life of an Amazon Warrior.

He advised me that the drone hasn't found the stealth gunboat yet, but they'll keep searching. *His statement worried me because we were not totally safe with that boat around.*

Sessions informed me of some good news. The entire Armed Forces were now in agreement to remove the President and Congress because of the Florida deal and the Chinese invasion. He stated that was the event that turned everyone against the President. The Military will set up a temporary government until new elections can be held. The entire U.S. Military would now move on Washington and remove the President and Congress from office. They would be placed under arrest and put on trial.

The Navy is sending ships to guard the Florida coast against any further Chinese incursions. In addition the Chinese government had been advised that the President over stepped his authority giving Florida to China. Therefore the agreement is null and void. Any further attempts to control Florida would be considered an act of war.

I asked him when a new government would be established. He had no time table because before any elections could be held the entire country needed to be cleaned up and order restored. The Army and Marines will be moving aggressively to do that. Curfews would be established in each city.

He told me the Green Zones will be removed and the Federal Police will be given a choice to join the Army or face prison time. Those Agents in command will be put on trial for crimes against the United States. People will be permitted to return to their homes if they so choose.

To sum it up, Sessions thinks it will take one or two years of martial law before things become more or less normal enough to have general elections.

I asked him to keep searching for the stealth gunboat and advised him we're going to put up a radar system.

Sessions informed me that there was a small portable radar system in the warehouse that was never set up because they didn't have the need for it. He gave me permission to use it.

He also told me that his Rangers would be moving south to remove any Red Chinese still in Key West. After that the Army will set up small garrisons around the state to establish law and order. He expects to return to Fort Desoto within another month or two. I wished him good luck.

END OF CONVERSATION

After talking to Captain Sessions I called my old buddy Rico. He answered the phone. "Rico here."

"Hey buddy, how's it going?" I asked.

"Jack, what's up?"

"Just calling to see how it's going."

"I thought you were coming back to help me out here."

I said, "I've been a little busy. The Red Chinese invaded here."

"What did you say? Red Chinese?"

"Yeah. Didn't you hear the President gave Florida to the Chinese for payment of the U.S. debt?"

"No. I'm out of touch here. When can you come over?"

"Two days from now. I'll tell you all about it then. That sound ok?"

"Yeah that sounds good. By the way, could you bring some ciprofloxacin along?"

I thought about this for a minute before responding. "What do you need that for?"

"I have a few people sick here."

"What are their symptoms?"

"Fever, diarrhea, vomiting, and pain."

"What do you think they have?" I asked.

"I don't know. At first I thought it was just food poisoning. I gave them all charcoal pills but it didn't help. Some of them have been sick for five days."

Activated pure charcoal powder is used in capsule form to absorb poisons and food poisoning from bacteria. A bacterium will bind to the charcoal and is then is removed from your body during bowel movements. This has been used for years in many hospitals. Some say it doesn't work, but I know for a fact that it does. It has saved my life a few times.

I said, "If they have a virus the ciprofloxacin won't help them. Let me talk to Doc Scott and see what he says."

Rico answered, "Alright, let me know what he says."

"Ok, will do."

Pushing the phone button off I lit up a smoke. There was a slight breeze blowing in from the northwest. I heard the birds and Fish Eagles chirping away as dusk was coming. I thought about what Rico told me. His people could have some type of flu or poison that the charcoal couldn't remove. It could be some type of blood poisoning.

I decided to stroll out into the bush and check on the two dead soldiers. I found body parts scattered about in the thick woods. It seems the pigs, coyotes, and other animals were having a feast. In a few days there would be nothing left of their corpses after the worms and maggots eat their share.

While standing there I remembered we left

the invisible suit that the commie used. I found it and jogged back to the truck since it was getting dark. Arriving at the field the kids and Hemmi were standing on the side of the road waiting for me.

After they jumped in I asked, "Well, did you kids learn anything?"

Shanda replied, "Yeah, we learned a lot. Now we know where our food comes from and how to grow it."

"It was pretty cool," Johnny commented.

We pulled up outside the Green Room. I advised Hemmi that I needed to talk to Doc Scott and have a drink or two. After that I'd come right home for dinner. She scooted into the drivers' seat and said, "Have two drinks and then come right home, Mister."

Johnny asked, "Can I come, Grandpa?"

"No you're too young. When you're eighteen I'll bring you to the bar."

"Eighteen. Gosh, that's too old!" Johnny replied, with a disappointed tone.

Too my surprise, Amy, Jim Bo, and Tommy, were in the bar already. Amy said, "Trini's funeral is all set for tomorrow. You'll be the second speaker after me. Jamie, Trini's boy-friend, is gonna speak after you."

I asked, "What time does it start?"

"It's at 10 am. Signs are posted on the bulletin boards telling everyone to show up. After the eulogies six Amazons and I will take her out to sea for burial using Jim's boat."

I grabbed a double shot of JD and chugged it down. "I gotta talk to the Doc about something. Amy, come with me since it's a medical problem."

"A medical problem? What's wrong?"

"I'll tell you over at Doc's."

We walked into his office to find Doc sitting in his big leather chair reading something on the computer. I said, "Doc, we need your help."

"Hi guys, what's up?"

"I'll tell you, but first super glue my two front teeth in so they can heal." It only took him a minute to fix my teeth so they wouldn't wiggle around. I didn't know if that would save them or not, but I had to try something.

"How's that?" Doc asked.

"Fine, I hope that saves them.

"I just talked to Rico on the phone and he has a few people that are sick. The symptoms are fever, diarrhea, vomiting, and pain. Rico gave them charcoal thinking it was food poisoning but it didn't help. What do you think?"

"How long they been sick?" Doc asked.

"Some have been sick for five days."

"Are any of them improving?"

"I don't think so."

"Well, if it's the flu they'd be recovering after five days. Let's see what happens in a few more days. Let's call Rico and talk to him," Doc suggested.

I pushed the quick dial button. He answered and I put him on the speaker. "Rico, I got Doc Scott here and Amy. They want to ask you some questions about the sick people there."

"Ok, shoot."

Doc asked, "Is any one getting any better?"

"Negative. Everyone seems to be getting worse."

Doc thought for a second and scratched his chin. "How many people are ill?"

"There're five that are really ill and four more that have fevers."

"It sounds contagious, so keep them isolated," Doc advised.

"They're isolated, but we still have to

provide proper care."

"Yes, of course, but have your people wear surgical masks and gloves."

"I would, but we don't have any. I need medical supplies ASAP."

Doc asked, "Jack, are there any medical supplies in the warehouse?"

"I think so, but I'll need to check it out."

Amy spoke up and asked Rico, "What are you doing with the waste and body fluids?"

"We burn the shit."

"Ok, that's good. Use a ten percent bleach solution to clean everything in the rooms."

Doc asked, "Is there anything else you can tell us about their symptoms."

Rico didn't reply right away. There was dead silence so Doc repeated. "Rico, is there anything else about their symptoms you can tell us."

"Yeah, I just noticed that one of them has blood in the diarrhea and urine."

Doc replied, "We'll be over with med supplies tomorrow after the funeral here. I'll do some more research and let you know what we might be dealing with."

"Ok thanks, Doc. See you guys tomorrow."

I hung up the phone. Doc looked at me and asked, "Do you remember the Ebola outbreak back in 2014."

My jaw dropped. I said, "Yeah, I thought that was contained."

Doc replied, "Ebola is never contained. Let me do some research and we'll talk tomorrow."

Doc is a computer geek and if anyone can research this he can.

Amy and I left the office and went for another drink at the Green Room. We sat over in a corner with Tommy and Jim. Amy told them about the problem at Rico's compound.

Amy said, "I hate to tell y'all, but this has the symptoms of Ebola."

I said, "If it's Ebola we can't let any new people on the island. Let's go home and discuss this tomorrow."

It was frightening that Ebola could be knocking at our door once again. None of us spoke on the way home.

In 2014 there was an Ebola outbreak in West Africa which quickly spread around the world due to air travel. Travelers took the disease everywhere on the planet. By 2016 it had made its way to the United States and thousands of people were being infected and dying. The hospitals were overwhelmed with sick people. They were full and if you caught Ebola there was an 80% chance you would die. The worst hit places were the southern Border States like Texas, Arizona, and California, but New York also became a hot spot. Then it started too slowly spread to other states as people ran from the epidemic.

By 2019 more than 3 million people had lost their lives to Ebola. The sad part was the government lied to us about how serious it really was. They kept it off the news and didn't reveal how many had died or how contagious this disease really was.

Finally sometime in 2020 a vaccine was invented and people in the Green Zones were given the anti-Ebola drug. Each person was also given a laser tattoo which proved they had taken the official vaccine. The tattoo showed an expiration date. To stay protected it was necessary to get a booster shot during the first five years.

Since Tocabaga was more or less isolated from the rest of the main land we never received the vaccine. We were rebels and the Federal Police didn't wanna mess with us.

I couldn't sleep thinking about the new threat we were facing. How are we going to combat something we can't see? A bug we can't detect. All our guns and security mean nothing against this enemy. We are fighting a new INVISIBLE enemy. This Invisible really had me worried about our future.

JULY 12, 2025

It was raining, a light drizzle, as we walked to the dock for Trini's funeral. It was a gloomy over-cast day, a fitting day, to bury one of our warriors. Amy was already there handing out the program to everyone.

I gave her a hug, took a program, and sat down with my family. I sat next to Doc Scott. Little Johnny was sitting on my other side, between me and his Dad. I looked at Doc, shook hands, and said, "You look like shit."

Normally Doc looks spic and span, clean as whistle, but now he looked tired and his clothes were wrinkled.

Doc whispered, "I was up all night researching the problem. After the funeral we need to talk." I nodded my head and looked at the program.

CELEBRATION OF LIFE FOR TRINI JONES

Pledge of Allegiance to the Flag

National Anthem

The Lord's Prayer

Eulogies and Speakers

21 Gun Salute

Final Farewells

I looked around and there were at least 400 people at the service. The rest were on guard duty or working. The services took about one hour and just as Trini's body was being loaded into the boat the sun broke out and the drizzle stopped. God must have been watching because a small rainbow appeared overhead. Everyone looked at it in awe.

As we watched the boat pull away Doc said, "Come to my office. I got something important to show you."

I replied, "Ok, I'll be there in a half hour." I walked away with my family.

After dropping my family off at home I drove to the medical office. As I walked in Doc said, "We got big trouble."

"Let me guess, Ebola," I replied.

"Yes, but it's worse than that."

"What could be worse than Ebola?"

"Well, let me explain. You know how sometimes you'd get a flu shot and then get the flu. Some kids got polio vaccines and ended up contracting polio. You know every year you need a new flu shot. You know for polio you need a booster shot."

"Yeah, I remember that."

"Ok, let's review what Ebola is. Read this from the CDC (Center for Disease Control) website

… www.cdc.gov/vhf/ebola."

"Symptoms of Ebola

- *Fever (greater than 38.6°C or 101.5°F)*

- *Severe headache*

- *Muscle pain*

- *Weakness*

- *Diarrhea*

- *Vomiting*

- *Abdominal (stomach) pain*

- *Unexplained hemorrhage (bleeding or bruising)*

Symptoms may appear anywhere from 2 to 21 days after exposure to Ebola, but the average is 8 to 10 days.

Recovery from Ebola depends on good supportive clinical care and the patient's immune response. People who recover from Ebola infection develop antibodies that last for at least 10 years.

Transmission

Because the natural reservoir host of Ebola viruses has not yet been identified, the manner in which the virus first appears in a human at the start of an outbreak is unknown. However, researchers believe that the first patient becomes infected through contact with an infected animal.

When an infection does occur in humans, the virus can be spread in several ways to others. Ebola is spread through direct contact (through broken skin or mucous membranes in, for example, the eyes, nose, or mouth) with

- *blood or body fluids (including but not limited to urine, saliva, sweat, feces, vomit, breast milk, and semen) of a person who is sick with Ebola*

- *objects (like needles and syringes) that have been contaminated with the virus*

- *infected animals*

- *Ebola is not spread through the air, or by water, or in general by food. However, in*

Africa, Ebola may be spread as a result of handling bushmeat (wild animals hunted for food) and contact with infected bats. There is no evidence that mosquitoes or other insects can transmit Ebola virus. Only mammals (for example, humans, bats, monkeys, and apes) have shown the ability to become infected with and spread Ebola virus.

Healthcare providers caring for Ebola patients and the family and friends in close contact with Ebola patients are at the highest risk of getting sick because they may come in contact with infected blood or body fluids of sick patients.

During outbreaks of Ebola, the disease can spread quickly within healthcare settings (such as a clinic or hospital). Exposure to Ebola can occur in healthcare settings where hospital staff are not wearing appropriate protective equipment, including masks, gowns, and gloves and eye protection.

Dedicated medical equipment (preferable

disposable, when possible) should be used by healthcare personnel providing patient care. Proper cleaning and disposal of instruments, such as needles and syringes, is also important. If instruments are not disposable, they must be sterilized before being used again. Without adequate sterilization of the instruments, virus transmission can continue and amplify an outbreak.

Once someone recovers from Ebola, they can no longer spread the virus. However, Ebola virus has been found in semen for up to 3 months. People who recover from Ebola are advised to abstain from sex or use condoms for 3 months."

"Ok, I read it. Now I know all about Ebola. So how is this different?"

"While I was researching Ebola I found that the government developed a vaccine called EV135. When they found out it was only good for five years they had to invent a booster shot."

"Yeah, I know that, but we never took it."

"Well, it's a good thing because vaccine EV135 is a ticking time bomb. After five years you need a booster before the expiration date otherwise you end up contracting a mutant form of Ebola."

"How do you know this?"

"I hacked into a Federal agency that I never heard of, called the DPC, or Disease and Population Control Agency. I found a Top Secret file about EV135 and EVB150 which is the booster shot. If you get the booster then you're Ebola free for life. If not then you'll die from the EV135 shot that you received or worse you'll live with it the rest of your live and suffer. You become a carrier passing it on to others. The EV135 contains a mutant semi-live Ebola virus."

"That's why they laser tattooed a date on your arm when you received EV135. Right?" I asked.

"Yes, that's right. If you don't receive the booster by that date you're a walking dead man."

"Why would the government do such a

thing?"

Doc replied, "Population control is the main reason because of food shortages and so forth. Stop and think about it; what better way to eliminate any enemies you have. All you do is make sure they don't get the booster shot."

"Holy, shit! You're right. The only ones left would be your loyal minions. You could be King and no one could stop you. I'll bet some of those people at Rico's compound took the EV135."

Doc replied, "I think you're correct. Call Rico and ask him if any of those infected have a date tattooed on their arm."

"Wait, before we call him, I have a question. Where can we get the EVB150 booster from?"

"According to the Top Secret Memo I read, it's being stored in secure locations around the country. I made a print out of the locations near us."

"What's the nearest location?" I asked.

"The Jacksonville or Miami Federal Reserve

Banks are the storage locations. The main one for the south eastern US is the Atlanta Federal Reserve. They move it from the banks to Green Zone clinics as needed."

"Why use the Federal Reserve Banks?"

"It's a no brainer. They have electricity, AC, armed security, and big strong vaults. They're impossible to break into."

"If we haven't taken the EV135 and we take the EVB150 vaccine will it kill us or make us immune to Ebola?"

Doc looked me in the eyes and said, "As far as I can tell it's safe to take the EVB150. Speaking for myself, I'm not taking any vaccine the government gives us."

"Yeah, I agree with you. We can't trust anything the government recommends. But if you already received the EV135 you have no choice. Before we call Rico let's run down to the warehouse and look for medical gear and hazmat suits."

Doc and I drove to the Fort and searched on the computer for the storage location of the medical supplies. We found everything we needed, rubber gloves, masks, and full hazmat suits along with disinfectant. We loaded up my truck and went back to his office.

I told him, "I think we should call Captain Sessions and advise him what you found. I don't know if his men have been given the EV135 or not."

"Go ahead and call him," Doc replied.

Before calling Sessions I thought carefully how to word what I would tell him. I pushed the speed dial and he answered, "Hello, Sessions here."

"Hello Captain, I am calling to advise a serious situation that Doc Scott discovered. Do you have a few minutes to discuss it?"

"Yeah, go ahead but make it brief."

"Well ... I'll try to make it brief. I received a call from Rico at his compound and it seems that a few of his people have contracted Ebola. Doc was doing research about it on the net and hacked into a Federal Agency called the Disease and Population Control Agency or DPC. He found a Top Secret memo about the vaccine EV135 and the booster shot called EVB150."

"I know about the vaccines, but never heard of the DPC. So what's the problem?"

"Did you know that EV135 isn't a safe vaccine? Five years after the inoculation date you develop full blown Ebola if you don't take the EVB150 booster vaccine."

"Are you sure?" Sessions asked.

"Yes, the Top Secret memo spells it all out. People who received EV135 will die within so many days, or weeks, five years after the inoculation date, if they don't obtain the booster shot. If they don't die, then they become infected carriers'. It sounds crazy, but it's true. Did any of your Rangers receive the EV135?"

"Thank God, no. My Rangers were ordered to take it, but they ran out of the vaccine before they got to us. I'm sure some of the other Rangers or other military branches did get the EV135, especially the ones based along the Mexican border."

I hesitated for a moment and told him, "Well, they need to get the EVB150 otherwise they're dead. Doc thinks this whole thing was a set up to control the population, and to terminate people who are dissidents or in disagreement with the President's actions. He wants to get rid of those who believe in the Constitution."

"I don't think SCOM has any of the EVB150," Sessions said.

"The EVB150 can be found at the Federal Reserve banks in Miami, Jacksonville, and Atlanta. Those are the distribution centers. The vaccine is taken from there to Green Zone clinics and given to those selected by the State who are deemed worthy of living."

Sessions commented, "I don't think the President deems the Army as worthy. He doesn't want us around to interfere with his plans. I agree it's a plot to eliminate any resistance."

"Yeah, you need to raid the Federal Reserve Banks and distribute the booster vaccine to all military personnel that you can. We're going to raid the Green Zone clinic in St. Petersburg and steal as much as possible."

"Jack, did any of your people take the first shot?"

"Not that I know of, but I need to check that. In any case, I never took it and I won't take the EVB150 either."

"What's the matter, you don't trust your own government?" Sessions inquired.

We both laughed out loud and I said, "Yeah, about as far as I can spit."

Still laughing Sessions said, "Ok Jack, thanks for the information. Have Doc email me the link to the memo from the DPC. I'm going to pass this on to SOCOM so they can move on it right away. Good luck and keep me posted."

After hanging up, Doc commented to me, "I'll bet the Army was one of the main targets they wanted to wipe out."

"Yep, you're right," I told him. "Let's call Rico and tell him we're on the way."

I called Rico and told him to check if anyone has a laser tattoo with a date on it. If they do, then they definitely have Ebola. We advised him we're leaving Tocabaga to bring him the medical supplies.

We arrived at Rico's compound with no problems. It was just Doc and me because I didn't want anyone else to be exposed. We pulled up to the front door, staying 50 feet away, and unloaded the gear onto the street.

Rico came out and started to walk over to us so I told him, "Don't come any closer." He was standing 15 feet away.

He stopped and said, "Yeah, you're right I don't want to infect you guys. I checked all my people and three of the nine have the tattoo."

"That confirms they have Ebola," Doc told him. "What about your other people, do they have a tattoo?"

"No one else has a tattoo. What can we do for the men that are infected?"

"Nothing except give them plenty of fluids and keep them isolated," Doc said. "We're going to try and find the EVB150 vaccine to give all your people to stop anyone else from coming down with it."

I told Rico, "We brought you all the med supplies we could. Just make sure you keep everything clean and disinfected. Wear the suits and clean them each time you come out of the room. By the way, how many people do you think have been exposed to those infected?"

Rico looked up at the sky, as if thinking, and replied, "I really don't know."

"Where are the infected people located now?"

"I moved them all to a small building away

from the others. I have five people taking care of them."

Doc advised him, "Your five men also need to be isolated from the others."

"It's a little too late for that isn't it?" Rico asked.

"No, it's not too late. If anyone comes down with a fever put them into isolation."

As Rico's men were moving the gear into the compound I told him, "Don't worry buddy. We're gonna mount a mission and find the EVB150 vaccine and bring some to you ASAP."

"Thanks for your help. Any idea when you'll get it?"

I thought about it and answered, "I hope in a few days. I'll call you when we find it."

Rico raised his hand goodbye as we mounted up and drove back to Tocabaga. *While driving I thought, maybe I'll never see my friend again. What a terrible way for a great warrior to die.*

I told Doc, "I can't let Rico die from Ebola." I smashed the pedal to the metal, speeding up to 65 mph, to let out the tension.

Arriving back at the Tocabaga Bridge it was about 6 pm. I stopped at the road block and told my guards if any outsiders come to the bridge don't have any contact with them. Stay at least 15 feet away because they may have Ebola. If they try to enter stop them but don't touch their bodies with your bare hands. Doc Scott gave the guards latex gloves to use.

Advising my men of the Ebola let the cat out of the bag. News would spread around Tocabaga like wild fire and could create a panic.

Rick was at the bridge and walked up to me and asked, "What the hell you talking about Ebola for?"

"We just came back from Rico's and nine of his men have Ebola."

"Did you come in contact with them?"

"Of course we didn't. We're not idiots. There's nothing to worry about."

Then Doc reminded me, "Jack, remember we did take in some people who were in the Green Zone a while back. They may have been given the EV135 vaccine."

"Shit you're right. Ok, here's what we're gonna do. I'll have the Amazons check every person for a tattoo just to be safe." I told Doc and Rick. "I'm gonna have a meeting about this at 9 am at the fire circle tomorrow. The Amazons can start checking people at the meeting."

"Ok, see you then," Rick replied, as we drove away.

While driving away I told Doc, "Let's draft up a memo about the meeting at your office so we can make copies. Then we'll post it." He nodded his head in agreement.

We drafted a memo and it simply read:

URGENT MEETING NOTICE

JULY 13, 2025 AT 9 AM.

ATTENDANCE IS MANDATORY

THE ONLY EXCEPTION IS FOR

SECURITY PERSONNEL ON DUTY

SUBJECT: NEW EBOLA THREAT

Doc Scott, Medical Director

Jack Gunn, Director of Security

I contacted Amy and asked her to have the Amazons post 100 copies around the island. While doing so, they should verbally advise as many people as possible.

I also asked that her warriors to visually check each person at the meeting for a laser tattoo. Each person checked would be stamped on the hand with the date using Doc's date stamp. The ink would stay on for a few days. It provided an easy way to verify if someone had been checked.

Doc and I were satisfied with the memo and there wasn't any more we could do. We went to the Green Room for a drink and then went home.

It was dark by the time I arrived home. I told everyone in my family, except the kids, about the Ebola plague at Rico's compound. Tommy, Jim Bo, Ron, and I went outside to discuss how to attack the Green Zone clinic.

It was decided that we would ask the Rangers to do a drone fly over when it was dark. The drone would provide us a live feed of the area. That way we could see, using infrared cameras, where the Federal Police were patrolling or stationed. The drone would fly over an hour before we would make our incursion.

Tommy suggested that two men should go on this mission. He selected himself and Army Mike. They were the best we had for a sneak and peek mission. They would be armed with silenced M4s and be wearing the Chinese Invisible combat suits. That would provide us the edge we needed to get in without being seen.

Pulling out a street map it was decided to enter the Green Zone using 3rd Avenue. Two Humvees with the 50 calibers would be used. Each truck would carry a driver, a 50 gunner, and one more man with a SAW riding shotgun.

The Hummers would sit outside the zone and wait for the call that the vaccine had been found. Then they would zoom in guns blasting away at anything or anyone in our way. We'd pickup the men, and steal all the med supplies possible.

Completing the mission plan I went to bed. I didn't sleep well thinking about the new INVISIBLE WAR we would be fighting. I'd rather be facing invisible soldiers than invisible bugs. I admit that Ebola scares the shit out of me.

JULY 13, 2025

I arrived at the meeting at 8:30 am and was pleased to see many people already there. Rick had set up a row of tables for the Board of Directors to sit at which faced the crowd of people.

I noticed the Amazons were already checking people as I went to the table to sit next to Rick. Rick shook my hand and said, "I'll open the meeting as usual and turn it over to you."

"Ok, I'll get right to the point. We don't want anyone to panic," I told him.

Tommy brought me a cup of coffee. I took a sip and found it was spiked with a shot of Jack Daniels. That was just what I needed to take off the edge. I hate talking to large groups of people. I chugged it down and asked him to bring me another. It also helped relieve my body pains.

Rick called the meeting to order promptly at 9 am and turned the meeting over to me. I don't remember exactly what was said, but it went something like this:

Dear Friends, as you probably already heard we defeated the Red Chinese Invisible Soldiers the other day. We're safe from them now. Good news is I was advised by Captain Sessions that the entire Military is in agreement to remove the President and the Congress. They'll install a new military government to restore law and order. It may take a few years before we can have normal elections again under the U.S. Constitution, but things are going to improve."

The crowd cheered, hooted, and whistled when they heard the news.

"That's the good news. The bad news is we are facing a new invisible enemy which is … Ebola. We found out, thanks to Doc's research, that anyone who received the EV135 Ebola vaccine is in danger. If you've taken this you're a walking time bomb. On your arm there's a date tattooed. That's your expiration date. The shot is good for five years, but after that date you will contract Ebola."

The crowd started to make a lot of noise and people were talking among themselves. I stopped speaking. Rick pounded the gavel and asked for order.

I yelled, "Please hear me out! You will contract Ebola if you do not receive the new EVB150 vaccine."

Someone yelled out, "Where do you get that from?"

I took a sip from my booze laced coffee and lit up a smoke while standing there. I paused a minute and took another drag on the cancer stick and replied while blowing out smoke. "You don't need the new vaccine if you never had the first one.

"If you were given the first vaccine please contact Doc Scott so we can issue you the EVB150 and save your life. We can't take the chance of you getting Ebola on Tocabaga. We're mounting a mission tonight to find the new vaccine so we have it on hand."

Rick stood up and commented, "This problem was caused by the President and his cronies. It was a plot to kill off the people who didn't agree with him."

I said, "The Amazons are checking everyone to see if you have a date on your arm. Anyone who has a date please step forward now."

The crowd was quite and everyone looked at

the person next to them. Finally after a few minutes one man stepped forward and raised his hand. It was Albert Madison, the retired Navy Medic.

Albert said, "I was given the vaccine. My date is July 15, 2025. That's just two days from now. What should I do, Jack?"

"Damn Albert, that's really cutting it close."

I yelled to the crowd, "Anyone else have a tattoo?" No one replied.

Amy approached me and said, "We finished checking everyone and it looks like Albert is the only one."

I thought that's a relief. There's only one person here to worry about.

The rest of the crowd started to slowly back away from Albert. Some yelled throw him off of Tocabaga. Many in the crowd began to leave the meeting.

I shouted, "Don't panic! Albert isn't contagious yet."

Someone screamed, "How the hell do you know?"

I pulled my gun and fired it into the air ... BAM ... BAM. Everyone stopped in their tracks and looked at me. I advised them, "We're going to obtain the new vaccine tonight and give it to Albert.

There's nothing to fear at this time."

I walked up to Albert and told him to go home and keep in isolation in one of his rooms. As Albert walked away with his wife and two kids the crowd parted to let him pass. They were afraid to touch him.

I continued speaking, "Starting today we're not letting any new people on Tocabaga. We don't know how bad this is going to get. I suggest no one leave the island for the time being. That's all I have to say."

I sat down and watched the people talking to each other. They were mumbling to each other and I could sense the fear in their faces.

Rick stood up and shouted, "Ok, the meeting is over! Go home and don't worry. Everything will be fine." Most left the meeting area, but a few stayed around to gossip.

I told Amy to post two Warriors at Albert's house just in case someone tried to hurt him or his family.

We went home for lunch and Army Mike came along to discuss the night mission. We had just finished eating lunch and sat down to make our final plans for the raid when I got a radio call from Maggie. "Jack, you better come to Shark Channel Bridge quick. Albert's here holding a gun to his head."

I told the group there's a problem with Albert, I'll be right back. I jumped in the truck and sped to the bridge as fast as possible. Albert was on the bridge, standing next to the guard rail, holding a gun. He was looking down at the water.

I slowly approached him and said, "Albert, what the hell you doing?"

"I know exactly what I'm doing, Jack. I was a Navy Medic and I've seen it all, including Ebola. It's too late for me."

"Maybe it's not. Let's talk about this."

Shaking his gun around in the air Albert said, "There's nothing to talk about. I don't wanna infect my family or anyone else. I don't wanna die from Ebola. It's a long painful death. I made my mind up what I need to do.

"Jack, promise me you'll take care of my wife and kids."

"Think about this. Don't do it, Albert."

"Promise me, damn it!"

"Ok, I promise!"

I was standing a few feet away from him. I could have grabbed his gun and stopped him but I froze. I didn't know what else to say. I couldn't speak as I watched Albert look up in the air and point the 357 magnum to the side of his head.

Albert looked at me and said, "Thanks, Jack."

I yelled, "Wait!"

It was too late. The blast blew the side of his head off and his body fell into the shark infested waters.

I looked over the side of the bridge as Maggie came running over. She peered down into the murky water and touched my hand. "There was nothing you could do," she said.

"Maybe not. If he was already infected then it's for the better. He took his own life to save his family and others on Tocabaga. He's a hero in my eyes." I made the sign of the cross and said a silent prayer.

I started to walk away. "I gotta go tell his wife and kids."

"I'll come with you," Maggie replied, as she ran after me.

We told Albert's wife and kids, but they already knew what he was going to do. Sue cried and said, "Albert was a good man."

I replied, "Yes, he was. He did the right thing. He did the honorable thing to protect his family and friends. Sue, if you need anything let me know. I promised Albert, I'd look after you and the boys. You have a lot of support here, so don't worry. I'll take care of arranging a memorial service in a few days." We gave her and the boys a hug and left without saying another word. What could we say?

We stopped at the clinic to advise Doc about Albert because they were close friends. Doc was shocked and said, "He was a good man and I'll miss him. He was a big help to me here at the clinic."

"Doc do you think he was contagious?" I asked.

"I don't think so, but I'll monitor his wife and kids' temperatures for 30 days just to be sure."

"What if they come down with Ebola?"

"I don't wanna think about that."

"Well we gotta think about it, so make up a plan just in case," I said.

"Alright, will do. I'll set up the memorial service if it's ok with you."

"That would be great. Thanks, Doc."

I asked Maggie, "You feel like going on a mission tonight to find the vaccine?"

"Yeah, count me in."

"Ok, let's go to my place. We're making up the plans now."

Maggie and I walked in the house with our heads hanging down. Mike asked, "What's wrong with Albert?"

"Albert killed himself. He was convinced that he already had Ebola. He didn't wanna infect anyone else so he blew his brains out and fell into Shark Channel," I told them.

No one said a word for a few minutes.

Mike asked, "Did he have it or not?"

I stated, "Doc doesn't think so but there's no way to tell now. Doc's going to monitor his family by checking their temperature for a month."

Everyone was silent again. I knew they were thinking the same thing as me. What if Albert's family does get Ebola?

Breaking the silence Tommy said, "We've finished the plans for the raid, so let's review them." He pulled out the city map and while placing it on the table he commented. "It's an easy plan and should be a cakewalk using the stealth suits."

He pointed to the map. "We take Interstate 275 to 22nd Avenue South, the gang zone. Hopefully we won't have any problems there. Then we head west to 3rd Street south and take it north. The trucks will stop at the old USF Business College and drop us off. You'll stay under cover until we radio you for pick up. We tuned your radios to the same frequency as ours."

I noticed that little Johnny was standing on the side of the room quiet as a mouse, but watching everything. He was a smart kid and liked watching us make the plans. Someday he would be doing the planning so I was happy he was taking an interest.

Tom continued, "As you know, the clinic is located on 3rd Street between Central Avenue and 1st Avenue North. Mike and I have a straight mile and a half walk to the clinic. Once we've found the vaccine you'll pick us up out front. Then we bug out and stay on 3rd Street heading north to 9th Avenue. At 9th Avenue we'll head west taking us to Route 19 and then home."

I asked, "What about the drone?"

Mike said, "The drone will be able to fly over one time at 1 am. It will give us a live feed so we can see where the patrols are located. Kick off time is 2 am."

Tommy butted in. "Truck one will have Tony driving, Jack on the 50 caliber, and Maggie on the SAW. Truck two has Chris driving, Jim Bo on the SAW, and Rick on the big gun."

I looked over at Jim Bo and asked, "Are you

up to this?"

He replied, "Yeah, my leg is fine. I can sit in a truck and fire a gun."

"What if something happens and you have to walk or run?"

Tommy commented back, "Then you'll have to carry him."

Everyone laughed at that comment, but I didn't. It was a serious question.

"Really, what's so funny? What if a Hummer gets disabled? What's Jim gonna do then?"

"I'll be able to keep up. If I didn't think so I wouldn't come along," Jim told me.

"If you say you're ok, that's fine with me."

"The key to this mission is speed. We need to get in and out as fast as possible. Once we radio you to pick us up the trucks have to move fast," Tommy advised.

"The plan looks fine to me. I agree speed is the key."

It was already 6 pm so I said, "Let's get some food and then get our gear ready."

After eating we checked and rechecked our weapons. I laid everything out on the table in the garage while Johnny watched me. He asked a lot of questions. What's this for? Why do you need that? How many bullets do you need? On and on he asked so many questions I couldn't think.

I did my best to answer his questions. It was important that he learn how to clean guns, know the type of ammo to use, and what equipment to take.

Johnny noticed that his Dad packed a glass cutter, a bolt cutter, and a small crowbar. He asked, "What's that for? Grandpa don't have those."

Tommy told him, "This is a glass cutter to cut windows, and this bar is used to pop open doors or windows. The bolt cutter is for cutting through locks. I may need these to break into the clinic."

I laughed because I remember teaching Tommy the same things. He's a good Dad spending the time teaching Johnny. Showing him how these tools worked was important training.

After three hours we finally had everything ready to go. We packed water, energy bars, and extra ammo into the Humvee. Tony checked the oil, coolant, gas, and tires. Tony had replaced the flat tire on the one Hummer. We were set to go.

It was 9 pm and Johnny went to bed. I suggested we get one drink before kickoff time to take off the edge. The four of us went to the Green Room and I poured a double JD for everyone.

Jim Bo asked, "What if Albert's family does get Ebola?"

"Yeah," Mike said.

I replied, "Doc told me he's gonna make up a plan just in case. But he's pretty sure Albert wasn't contagious."

"I don't want pretty sure. I want 100 percent sure," Tommy stated.

"Yeah, me too," I advised. "But if they get Ebola what should we do? Shoot them? We'll have to wait and see what happens. They're in quarantine for 30 days."

I held up my glass and stated, "Cheers. Here's to a safe mission." We clinked glasses and downed the booze. I lit up a smoke and asked the group, "After we pick up the vaccine how about we run some over to Rico's compound before coming home."

Everyone agreed with that idea as long as we weren't being chased by the Feds. We went home and waited for 1 am when the drone would fly over the Green Zone. We did one more check on our gear right before midnight.

JULY 14, 2025

AFTER MIDNIGHT

Eight of us where sitting outside on my patio, when the cell rang. The Drone Master provided us a live feed of the flight over the Green Zone. We could see, using infrared, the locations of each Federal Officer.

Between the drop off point and the clinic there were only 8 guards posted. In addition there was one roving patrol, using a vehicle, which passed by the clinic about every 30 minutes.

It was almost 2 am when we mounted up and headed off Tocabaga driving with our headlights off. We arrived at the 22nd Avenue exit and stopped to scan the street for bad guys. This was gang territory. It had always been gang-infested, even in the good times. These gangs were well armed and dangerous. They would kill you just for fun.

Looking through our night vision it seemed all clear so we proceeded forward at a high rate of speed. Our weapons were loaded, ready to rock and roll.

Speeding down the street at 60 mph we reached 3rd Street in 10 minutes with no problems. On the corner of 3rd and 22nd sat my Father's old house. I looked at it as we drove by. I wondered if anyone was inside using it for shelter. I hoped not because that was still family property.

It was a short 5 minute ride to the drop off point. We found the area was all clear and no Free Roamers were about. We parked the trucks behind some over grown bushes next to an old office building. The building protected one of our flanks.

We all dismounted and helped Mike and Tom put on the stealth uniforms, while Maggie and Jim Bo provided security. They placed the cloth covered helmets over their heads and turned invisible.

I heard Tommy say, "Radio check."

Mike answered back, "Copy you A-ok."

I heard their voices on my radio and replied

back, "Copy you both."

There was a half moon out so it wasn't completely pitch black. Mike and Tommy took off the helmets and we wished them good luck. Tommy said, "When you hear us say ... Ebola is ready. Come and get us."

I said, "Got it ... Ebola is ready." I handed them their guns and tools.

Putting the helmets back on; they disappeared into the darkness. I couldn't help but worry about my only son. I said a silent prayer for their safety. Now we had to wait.

I estimated that it would take them about 30 minutes to cover the mile and a half. Depending on the situation it may take another 30 minutes to find the vaccine. So the total time would be 60 to 90 minutes at most. I noted the time on my watch.

I commented, "Alright everyone. Stay on your toes and keep alert. You never know when a Free Roamer could be around. There's probably some inside this building watching us right now."

This area was very close to the spot where I rescued Rosie and her brothers from three dirtbags. I knelt down and scanned the whole area using naked eyes and then with my night vision. Using the FLIR I did see two targets about 400 yards away near the next building. It was pretty much all open ground between us and them so we could keep track of them.

I told Maggie, "At 2 o'clock there're two bogies. Watch them."

Nodding her head, she looked through the FLIR, and said, "I see them."

Thirty minutes later Maggie said, "Boss, there's more than two now. There's a bunch of them."

I quickly spun around on my knee and peered through my scope. She was right. There were now six men gathered in that location. They were standing there and seemed to be talking.

I softly told my crew, "Six bad guys at 2 o'clock. If they come within 100 yards take them out. Don't fire until I give the order. Use your silenced M4s cause we don't what the Feds to know we're here."

I checked the time. Forty minutes had gone by so I radioed the sneakers. "Hey, how's it going?"

The radio hissed and Mike replied, "We're at the clinic trying to get inside. We had to wait for a patrol to pass."

"If you can, hurry it up. We got company here."

"Who is it?"

"I don't know for sure. Probably Free Roamers. There's six of them."

"Only six. Shit that shouldn't be a problem for you guys. Just let Maggie handle them," Mike told me. "We're going as fast as we can." I laughed, but it was true, Maggie could kill them all.

"Roger that."

"Tony, are they still coming our way?" I asked.

Before he could reply, Maggie said, "Yes. They're about 150 yards out."

"I concur that," Tony responded.

"Jim Bo, watch our left flank. Chris, watch our backs. Rick watch everything," I whispered. "Let's start picking these guys off."

I fired a round hitting one dirtbag. He fell to the ground. Maggie fired next hitting her target and then Tony. Two more men dropped dead. The rest of them fell to the ground to keep from being shot. They were hiding in the deep grass making it impossible to target them.

Not one of them returned fire which in my mind meant they couldn't see us. They knew our general location but didn't have an eye ball on any one of us. The question was would they crawl forward in the thick high grass or retreat?

Jim Bo softly shouted, "We got company coming on the left flank."

"How many?" I asked.

"I think five men. They're next to the building, across the street."

"If they try to cross the street terminate them," I replied.

These guys could have us in a cross fire. I wondered what kind of weapons they had. In any case I was hoping that we'd get the radio call soon so we could move out.

I wasn't worried about this bunch of bad guys. I knew we could handle them. We could kill them all if we needed too. I just didn't want any of my people to get killed.

I looked at the time and 90 minutes had gone by. What the hell is holding them up? I lit up a smoke and tried to relax. *I was thinking, come on Tommy hurry up.*

Rick said, "Jack, we got four more men approaching from 12 o'clock."

I looked through my scope. They were right in front of us about 50 yards away. The Roamers were blocking the direction we needed to go.

"Rick, start shooting!" I said.

Just then my radio crackled, "Ebola is ready. Hurry up we're trapped inside the clinic by the Feds. They don't know we're here because they can't see us, but they know someone broke in the clinic."

I shouted, "Everyone, mount up. Ebola is ready." My crew jumped up and scrambled to the Humvees.

After everyone was in position I told them to shoot anyone and everything in our way. The motors fired up and my truck took the lead. Pulling out from behind the bushes I broke the silence of the night by firing the big 50 caliber machine gun at every man I saw. I could hear the other truck's 50 firing also. Maggie was shooting out the side window at targets she could see. The noise was deafening. Fire was spitting out of the barrels lighting up the night.

I shouted to Tony, who was driving, "Floor it!" The Hummers roared away from the Free Roamers as some of their rounds pinged off the bullet proof trucks.

Standing in the gun turret I was bouncing around like a bobble head. The street was rough and full of pot holes from years of no maintenance. I stopped shooting and had to hold on, with both hands, to the grab handles to keep from flying out.

We were approaching the first Federal check point located at 4th Avenue. I could see two SUVs and four guards looking in our direction. The SUVs were kinda blocking the street, but not fully because there was about a six foot gap between them. The Fed agents were standing behind them. Bullets started to hit the front of our vehicle so I grabbed hold of the machine gun and started to fire back.

I looked down and saw Maggie hanging halfway out of the side window shooting her SAW. She pulled back inside just as our truck rammed into both SUVs banging them out of the way. I yelled at her, "Keep your ass inside the truck!"

The SUVs went flying from the impact striking the agents. It knocked them down like bowling pins. I turned around to see Hummer two zoom in between the SUVs. Rick swung his turret and shot at anyone who was still standing. They didn't know what hit them.

It was only another 3 blocks to the clinic. The street is six lanes wide here, so truck two pulled up on our left-side. The Hummers were running side-by-side so we both could see what was ahead. We saw two Federal trucks in front of the clinic. I estimated that meant we could be facing up to eight men.

There were four standing outside near their vehicles in the street. They heard us coming and looked in our direction as we were now only one block away. We opened up on the bastards. The machine gun rounds ripped through the SUVs dropping all four men in a few moments.

Apparently the men inside the clinic heard the gunfire and came running out. Seeing us they moved behind their trucks and opened up. We came to a tire screeching stop about 100 feet away and all six of us fired on the four Federal stooges.

As the gun battle raged I saw the agents fall to the ground one by one. Tommy radioed me, "We killed some of the Feds for you. Pick us up." It seems that Mike and Tommy were able to get out of the clinic in the invisible suits and gun these guys down from behind.

As we pulled up to the clinic they took off their helmets and Mike yelled, "Come on give us a hand there's a lot of stuff here." Tony and Chris helped carry the drugs out while we provided security.

It seems we hit the jack-pot stealing 30,000 doses of vaccine and other much need medical supplies such as antibiotics. The supplies filled up the back of both Hummers.

After about 5 minutes we quickly departed heading straight down 3rd Street. There was one more Fed check point to pass through which was on

5th Avenue. They wouldn't be expecting anyone coming from this direction. They wouldn't be expecting speeding trucks coming from downtown with machine guns spitting fire and death.

They must have heard the gun battle because they were expecting us. As soon as they saw us they started shooting. I could see the bright muzzle flashes from their weapons. We returned fire as their bullets sparked and bounced off our trucks.

These guys, lucky for us, were stupid, because they were standing out in the open. They didn't even try to hide behind their trucks or a tree. The wall of machine gun fire cut them down leaving four bloody bodies in the street.

We drove quickly around the road block, and went to 9th Avenue. Stopping there I asked, "Is everyone ok?" All replied they were ok. That was a relief for me. I glanced behind us to see if we were being followed. Thank God, it was all clear.

We dismounted and took a break. I was sipping some water as Mike and Tommy took off the rest of the stealth clothing.

Tommy said, "We cleaned them out."

"I'm just happy the mission went well and no one was injured. Let's go to Rico's," I said. We jumped in the trucks and headed to Rico's as planned.

Pulling up to the 54th Avenue Bridge we could see the compound was on fire so we stopped. Flames were shooting high into the air lighting up the night sky. It was burning out of control. I got on the phone and called Rico but there was no answer.

Chris asked, "What now?"

Tommy said, "It looks like the whole place is on fire."

I instructed everyone, "We'll pull up as close as we can. If anybody comes up to the trucks don't let them touch you."

Mike asked, "Should we shoot them?"

"If they get too close shoot them."

The fire was so hot we stopped at 200 feet away. I told everyone to stay put while I went to check it out.

I managed to move within 100 feet of the front door to the main building but the heat was too intense. I couldn't move any closer. I saw some shadows of people running away from the fire in the other direction. Then two men and a woman came running over to me. Their clothes were burned in places and maybe their bodies. I couldn't tell because of the black soot on their faces and hands.

They were within 15 feet of me when I pointed my gun in their direction. I warned them not to come any closer. They stopped in their tracks.

I asked, "Have any of you seen, Rico?"

One of them said, "Hey, aren't you, Jack Gunn?"

"Yeah. What the hell is going on here?"

"They're killing everyone. Please let us go, we don't mean you any harm," the woman replied.

I lowered my M4 and they took off running. I shouted, "Who's killing everyone?" They kept running and didn't look back.

I moved closer to the fire and yelled, "Rico … Rico!"

I stood there holding my hand up to cover my face from the heat. I yelled again for my friend. I could see people running around inside the compound trying to escape. They were trying to climb the razor wire fence.

I stood there as long as I could and then backed away from the heat. I heard several explosions and the crack of bullets going off from the heat. I noticed dead bodies lying on the street. They appeared to have been shot, but I couldn't tell. I sure as hell wasn't going to touch them because they might be infected.

Suddenly the 10 foot high fence collapsed from the heat and five men rushed out at me. When they came within 20 feet I warned them. "Stop! Don't come any closer or I'll shoot."

They didn't respond, so I started too slowly back away from them. They looked like zombies walking towards me. They were in shock for sure. I yelled again but they kept coming. Moving backwards I tripped over something in the street and landed on my ass.

When I fell the five men rushed towards me. I scrambled, managing to swing my M4 in their direction, and opened fire on full automatic. I sprayed rounds back and forth, as they dropped to the ground five feet away. I kept scooting backwards, on my butt, to make sure I was out of their reach.

That was too close for comfort. Thank God, none of them touched me. I breathed a sigh of relieve, stood up, and brushed the soot off my pants. I wondered if they were trying to kill me, take my gun, or what.

I yelled some more for Rico. After half an hour of yelling and peering into the flames I walked back to the vehicles. I told everyone, "Let's get the hell out of here! I couldn't find Rico. Maybe he's dead."

No one said a word as we drove back to Tocabaga except for Tommy and he asked, "What do you think happened?"

I responded, "I don't know. I just don't know."

We arrived back on Tocabaga and put the vaccine in a refrigerated storage unit.

The eight of us went to the Green Room for a much needed drink. Tony poured us all a double shot. We held up the glasses for a toast and looked at each other not saying a word. After downing the booze, I said, "Good job guys. I'm beat, see y'all later."

I went home, took a shower, and went to bed. Just as it was turning daylight, I crawled into bed trying not to wake my wife. She softly asked me, "You ok?"

"Yeah, I'm ok. I just need some sleep." She lightly rubbed my shoulder; the one that always hurts from the fight I had with al-Qaida terrorists. Ever since I fell into a 10 foot pit it has never been the same. I am in pain most of the time when I raise my left arm.

I'm glad she didn't ask me any more questions because I didn't feel like talking. I didn't want to think about what happened to Rico or I'd never fall asleep.

I closed my eyes and tried not to think about

the new Invisible enemy.

That's all for now.

GOD BLESS AMERICA, LAND OF THE FREE, and HOME OF THE BRAVE

Jack Gunn

Email: Tocabaga.jack@gmail.com

DRAMATIS PERSONAE

Albert Madison – Navy Vet. who comes to Tocabaga with wife and two kids

Army Mike – Retired Army combat vet, we just call him Mike.

Barry – A quisling killed by the Gunn family

Billy – Kid found living on the street with his sister Rosie and brother Peter

Brogan – A Tocabaga security guard who went MIA

Bok Lam – A Chinese man and close friend of Jack's since high school

Buck – Motorcycle gang leader killed by Maggie

Chase – A quisling

Colonel Turner – Commanding Officer of the Army Rangers based at Fort   Desoto

Colonel Park - aka Captain Kim a South Korean spy working for China

Corporal Phillips – In charge of the communications office at Fort Desoto

Captain Sessions – Combat officer, commands and controls combat   operations in the field

Captain Riley – Female tank commander, girl

friend of Captain Sessions

Captain Zhu Lei – A commie killed by Tommy

Chris – Tocabaga security guard and close friend of Jack

Dew – A quisling killed by the Gunn family

Dr. Carl Urban – The inventor of the RCCD Units and friend of Jack's

Dr. Carl Urban, Jr. – Son of Dr. Urban

Dr. Alvin Sinclair – Robot inventor and Commie killed by Jack

Ellen – A lonely woman

First Lt. Fisher – TALOS Warrior, Platoon commander

Farmer John – An old farmer saved by Jack, now living on Tocabaga

Guy Allen or GA – Suspected spy living on Tocabaga was killed by Jack

General Chen – A Red Chinese Army General in charge of the Florida invasion force

General Harper – Commander of the Rangers located at SOCOM

George Taylor – A nice kid who was bullied in school by Nick

Hemmi – Wife of Jack Gunn

Joe – RCCD tech. Supervisor; a tough guy killed by Jack

Little Johnny – Adopted grandson of Jack's

Johnny the Fisherman – A quisling killed by security

Jill – A warrior killed by Feds

Jim Bo – Husband to Amy and son-in-law of Jack

Jimmy Smith – A bully from years ago

Ken – US Deputy Marshal who went missing

Leroy – The man who killed Jack's little brother Mike

Lee – A Chinese invisible

Mike – Jack Gunn's little brother killed by a doper

Maggie – Wife of Robbie, who is in charge of the farming

Mr. Johnson or Famer John – Old time Farmer

Mr. Horn – Pig farmer and dirt bag who wanted to kidnap Maggie for   breeding

Nick – A bully from Junior High School

Peter – Little nine year old brother to Rosie

Rosie – A fifteen year old girl Jack found living on the street

Robbie – Best friend of Jack Gunn, a Tocabaga

security guard killed by the FPF on April 27, 2025

Ron – Brother of Jack Gunn Retired Navy vet. Part of Tocabaga security.

Rick – President of Tocabaga Association, security team member

Sally – A warrior killed by Feds

Scotty – A quisling killed by security

Sergeant Hammer – Army Ranger

Sergeant First Class Dale – killed in action

Sergeant Major Willis – Ranger squad leader and security guard for Jack

Sergeant Cain – the Drone Master

Sergeant Smith - Army Ranger assigned as security guard for Jack

Stan – Deputy Marshal

Sue – Wife of Albert Madison

Tommy Gunn – Son of Jack Gunn and a retired Marine Scout Sniper

Tony – Bar keeper and sharp-shooter for Tocabaga security

Trini – Amazon Warrior who killed Troy

Troy – A quisling killed by security

Victor Elway – An old farmer from Ellenton now living on Tocabaga with his friend Farmer John

Zack – A quisling killed by the Gunn family

OTHER BOOKS BY THOMAS H. WARD

THE TOCABAGA CHRONICLES:

TOCABAGA 1: Revised Edition

TOCABAGA 2: Theoterrorism

TOCABAGA 3: Warm Blood – Cold Steel

TOCABAGA 4: The Talos Warriors

TOCABAGA 5: The Quislings & Androktones

TOCABAGA 6: The Dimachaerus Clan - Missing In Action

TOCABAGA 7: Pàn Guó Zuì - High Treason

TOCABAGA 8: The Invisibles

CONTACT THOMAS H. WARD:

Website: www.ThomasHWardBooks.com
Email: Tocabaga.Jack@gmail.com
Facebook: www.Facebook.com/Tocabaga

www.ingramcontent.com/pod-product-compliance
Lightning Source LLC
Chambersburg PA
CBHW051520170626
46811CB00002B/919

* 9 7 8 0 6 9 2 3 3 7 9 3 6 *